"Quiet probe?" Carl Lyons said. "Let's do it," Blancanales nodded.

They signaled the two British soldiers to back off. Able Team lay prone, modified Colts held at full extension; accuracy was essential. They aimed into the darkness of the field.

The three autopistols, set for single shots, sneezed three .45-caliber bullets.

Two terrorists spun quickly, their mouths and throats ripped away. A third fell straight back with a hole above his eyes.

Then the next trio of slugs hit home. One crushed a larynx, another an eye that it drove into the brain. The third slug hit the bridge of a nose.

Corpses fell silently to the soft earth.

The three Americans had created their opening.

Now they went through it, into the blackness.

Mack Bolan's
ABLE TEAM

Mack Bolan's
PHOENIX FORCE

ABLE TEAM

Royal Flush

Dick Stivers

A GOLD EAGLE BOOK FROM

W🌐RLDWIDE

TORONTO • NEW YORK • LONDON • PARIS
AMSTERDAM • STOCKHOLM • HAMBURG
ATHENS • MILAN • TOKYO • SYDNEY

First edition February 1984

ISBN 0-373-61210-9

Special thanks and acknowledgment to
Stephen Mertz for his contributions to *Early Fire*.

Printed in Canada

"If gallantry gives way to anonymous refuge behind supersonic weapons, the days of personalized war are gone forever."

—*Ontario Lieutenant Governor John Black Aird*

OPERATIONAL: IMMEDIATE
FROM: US EMBASSY/LONDON
TO: BROGNOLA/STONY MAN OPS
STICKER SENDS

RELIABLE SOURCE INDICATES TWO HUNDRED
KILOS HIGH GRADE COCAINE NOW IN TRANSIT X
DESTINATION=NYC
ARRIVAL=IMMINENT
SHIPMENT ABOARD PANAMA FREIGHTER
CANAL QUEEN X SHIPMENT BEING BROUGHT
IN BY JOHN MCELROY X MCELROY SHOULD
GIVE SOLID LEAD TO SHILLELAGH
END

PROLOGUE

Two hundred kilos—roughly ten million dollars at wholesale levels. By the time it got to the streets it would be worth at least three times as much. The Drug Enforcement Agency would love to get that kind of a bust, and Stony Man's Hal Brognola was going to give it to them—with a string attached.

John McElroy was a leader in the Irish National Army of Liberation—NAL—an offshoot of the IRA. The organization specialized in terrorist attacks in England, always in large crowds. Their civilian body count was in the hundreds. In one attack, when the former Secretary for State for Northern Ireland was assassinated in a massive bomb blast in a crowded soccer stadium, a stampede of panicked spectators tried to flee the scene, doubling the number of dead.

In all, the NAL was responsible for killing and crippling more than three hundred people.

McElroy's primary function within the NAL was that of fund raiser. Increasingly, the terror-mongers in Ireland had had to resort to smuggling drugs and guns to fill their war chests.

He was an engaging man, according to intelligence files, and a talented organizer. These talents allowed McElroy to build one of the major drug-distribution rings in Britain, the profits from which went to finance NAL activities. The anticipated foray into the American market represented a major expansion of McElroy's activities.

"Sticker" was a gutsy guy named Leopold Turrin. Leo was Mack Bolan's closest friend and, along with Hal and April and Jack Grimaldi, his most valuable Stony Man ally independent of Able Team and Phoenix Force. At one time, during the initial struggle at Pittsfield, Bolan had sworn he would execute Leo Turrin, Mafia underboss with the "girls franchise" in western Massachusetts, blood nephew to Sergio Frenchi, the boss of the Berkshires. But Bolan had learned just in time that Leo "The Pussy"—Sticker—was an undercover federal agent, a soldier of the same side. Leo became a total convert to Bolan's cause, an invaluable insider. So began a lifetime commitment to advise and assist Mack Bolan and his men along their every brawling mile, a commitment that would be forged the stronger by the kind of betrayal and bereavement that could hit the Stony Man program at any time and expose them all to the highest winds of horror.

Officially, Leo was in London to advise the Criminal Investigation Department of Scotland Yard on a growing organized crime problem experienced in the United Kingdom. The request had come through channels for the best available help on the problem. Sticker was the best available.

To protect the undercover Fed, arrangements had been made to fly him to Britain on a military jet, pass him through customs and immigration with his face wrapped in bandages, and install him in a "gilded cage"—a secure area of the U.S. Embassy.

The *un*official reason for Leo being in London was Shillelagh. For some months now, indications of disturbing problems in the British counterterrorist efforts had filtered through to American intelligence. The agency responsible for the British efforts was COATUK—the Committee on Anti-Terrorism in the United Kingdom. The committee had representatives from CID, the Secretariat of State for Northern Ireland, MI5, and the SAS.

It appeared that the Irish terrorists also had a representative on COATUK—an infiltrator. The indications of the "Irish representative" were scattered. Considered as a whole, they pointed to a major systematic sabotage of counterterrorist efforts.

Because nothing was certain—including who could be trusted within COATUK—the Americans could say nothing to their British counterparts. With the request from CID for Sticker, a man who had served with the Special

Forces in Vietnam and who knew what could happen when men faced rampant corruption, an opportunity was handed to Stony Man to check out Shillelagh.

Able Team had just returned, bloodied and exhausted, from Honduras in their continued pursuit of Central American fascists. They needed a change of scene, particularly Carl Lyons who made a statement on the guerilla wars: "I'm sick of killing teenagers." Senior specialist Rosario "Pol" Blancanales, electronics wizard Hermann "Gadgets" Schwarz and ex-LAPD hotshot Carl "Ironman" Lyons represented the final option wherever civilization was threatened, and it was impossibly tough work. A working visit to one of the sources of modern civilization might help to heal some wounds, even as it threatened to create new ones.

The image of modern Britain was cavalry guardsmen lying dismembered in the street, gore smearing their chromed breastplates in the shock-numbed aftermath of a terrorist bomb that settled like a pall on scenery once associated with pomp and circumstance. Innocent people by the score had been murdered in these episodes.

The men of Able Team were ready to do war. Events dictated that they fly into action far from the urban hunting grounds of Los Angeles and the hellgrounds of Central America. The siren had sounded and the specialists had heard that special call—they would be abroad tonight for sure. . . .

But first New York, and the string attached to Hal's gift of two hundred kilos of coke.

1

The sentry at the side door of the warehouse emitted a gasp as the apparition of black materialized from the fog.

"That's the last sound you make," the attacker advised. The edge of death was in his voice.

Al Capri looked wistfully at the shotgun he'd leaned against the wall only a moment ago. He raised his empty hands slowly in the air, examined the deadly apparition more closely.

The man was just a touch over six feet tall and well-muscled. From the top of the wool cap to the crepe-soled shoes, he was in black and dressed to kill. Two military bandoliers crisscrossed his chest, holding the munitions for war; around his neck, a compact submachine gun hung by a strap. At the moment, Al's biggest worry was the autopistol aimed at his chest.

"On the ground, spread-eagled," growled the voice.

The mafioso complied and he was soon secured by plastic riot cuffs extracted from a pocket in the skintight blacksuit. A piece of adhesive tape across Capri's mouth ensured his silence.

Elsewhere in the gloom, two more sentries greeted the other two members of Able Team.

Able Team. All three men were rigged for silent combat. The autopistols were Colt Government Models. Armorers had increased the twist of the Colt's rifling to reduce the slug's speed to subsonic levels and greatly increase the weapon's accuracy. The ten-round magazine could be emptied one shot at a time or in precise three-round bursts with a flick of the selector lever.

The Ingram Model 10 SMG was the "firefight" weapon this mission. Equipped with a MAC suppressor, the weapon itself was silent. The target heard the crack of the bullet, but by that time it was too late. The firing rate had been reduced from 1200 rounds per minute to a more manageable 700, but even with that modification, the formidable weapon could deliver its thirty rounds of .45-caliber ammunition in less than three seconds on full autofire.

The men's radios were Gadgets Specials. From the control box containing the circuits and transmission button, two wires were fed underneath the skinsuit, one terminating in a small throat mike, the other in a compact earplug. The range was limited, but entirely suitable for close-quarter operations.

The DEA had had the *Canal Queen* under surveillance from the moment she docked the previous afternoon. Now Able Team waited patiently as the cargo was cleared through customs and brought to the warehouse.

The small building was owned by Johnson & Associates—Importers. The company was a front operation for one Paul Scaramelli. A wholesale distributor of narcotics, Scaramelli had ambitions to be the major importer of narcotics into the New York area. This deal was a major stepping-stone in achieving those ambitions.

The fog had rolled into the Hudson River dockyards earlier in the evening, isolating the warehouse from its neighbors. Half an hour later, two limousines rolled up to the building, disgorging a hard patrol of hired protection. Most of the newcomers went inside, leaving sentries to guard the three entrances to the building.

The DEA agents had radioed this information to the agent in charge and pulled back on his instructions to let Able Team in.

CARL LYONS TOOK A LAST LOOK at Al Capri, then moved to the door to the building and entered. He hit his transmit button once.

His entrance did not go unnoticed, but as one of McElroy's hardmen reacted to the intruder, Lyons's silenced auto-pistol coughed once. The slug caught the man just below his nose. The faceless nonbeing let go of its AK-47. The weapon clattered to the floor. Lyons scooped it up.

Scaramelli and McElroy stood examining the goods stashed in two crates at the far end of the warehouse. Moments earlier, the Irishman had placed a call that confirmed the deposit of eight million American dollars in a Swiss numbered account. Paul felt good about the deal, very good, and prepared to set up a subsequent deal with the Irishman. The clatter of the assault rifle startled the two men.

Mafiosi and terrorists opened fire on the source of the sound. Lyons had found shelter among stacked crates, part of the cargo from the *Canal Queen*, as bullets tore into the position he had abandoned a heartbeat earlier.

Gadgets used the diversion to enter the warehouse through the rear side door. The inside sentry had no idea of the extent of the invader's shooting skill. His head exploded. Gadgets moved quickly to a gap between two stacks of crates and climbed till he could see his partners' positions.

The warehouse was about one hundred fifty feet long and thirty feet high. The owners and protectors of the white powder hid among the crates. Now the rolling booms of heavy shotguns punctuated the staccato of automatic-weapon fire and the sharper reports of small handguns. The fire was directed toward Lyons's position.

Gadgets unslung the Ingram from around his neck and brushed the trigger, sending a short burst into two men whose cover behind stacked crates he had exposed. Small puffs of white powder kicked up as the .45 whizzers perforated a load of crated plastic bags. The fire cut down one of the two men in a lethal stream of .45 tumblers as the second man spun away from the white puffs and scrambled for the left side of the warehouse—only to feel the 230-grain kickers find him and turn his scramble into a sprawl.

Gadgets had no trouble picking up McElroy. His shock of unruly blond hair was moving toward the main entrance of the warehouse, progressing crate by crate. Gadgets radioed the information to Blancanales.

Scaramelli, too, had spotted the target's retreat. Paul Scaramelli had worked his way up from a runner in the late Freddie Gambella's family. A lot of changes happened when Freddie fell to Mack Bolan. Paul had managed over the years to come up on the right side of the interfamily wars that had erupted, and he'd slowly built a solid power base in New York. One of the things he had learned was to protect his assets, which he was doing right now. No little shit of a foreigner was going to leave Paul holding the bag.

"You Irish son of a bitch. You take one more step and you're dead!" the Mafia slimebucket hollered at the retreating terrorist. The reply to the challenge was a burst from McElroy's AK-47.

Scaramelli died protecting his assets. Gadgets watched from above, saw vital juices pump out onto the floor.

McElroy's victory was short-lived. A blast of shot from one of Scaramelli's tagmen found the Irishman's back near point-blank range. The dead terrorist folded quietly like a sail falling when the wind stops.

"The pigeon is dead," Gadgets told his partners. The signal removed any cautionary restraints on Able Team.

Lyons had been moving slowly away from his original cover, dashing across the small aisles between the stacks of crates, seeking a better firing line. Now he opened up with the appropriated AK-47, sending 7.62mm tumblers through a gap between crates. The gap was narrow, but the bullets negotiated it and shredded flesh as they plowed into the gunner beyond.

From his position among crates at the front of the building, Blancanales saw two men working their way beneath Gadgets's perch.

With his Colt in a two-handed grip, Blancanales terminated one-half of the threat, but bullets meant for the second man were still being absorbed by the first when the fleeing guy gained cover.

"Watch it, Gadgets, I only hit one of them," Blancanales relayed through his throat mike.

A head popped up over the crates in front of Gadgets. The Wizard sheared it off with a stream of bullets aimed at eye level. The anatomy that remained landed on the floor with the heavy crumple of wet laundry.

Retreating gunmen came to a stop as a barrage of bonecrushers hit them from three directions. They retreated into death.

Silence descended on the scene, and the smoke and smell of cordite slowly dissipated. Able Team worked its way out from cover, then searched the interior of the warehouse for survivors.

Finding none, the three assembled at the corpse of the man they had come to get. Blancanales searched McElroy's pockets, found a hotel key and a few scraps of paper.

The three men took a last look around at the carnage.

As they emerged, they were observed by Al Capri, a sentry Lyons had spared in determined defiance of his reputation as crowd killer. The cuffed and gagged Capri had heard the sounds of the raging battle. One glance at the grim faces of the three men down there told him that life was a sweet and precious thing. He thanked a few saints for the compassion of the tall one with blond hair.

2

Ripper Dan Aliotto pulled away from the curb at Terminal Three, Heathrow Airport, London. Resting beside him in the front seat of the ambassador's limousine were the three black leather cases that the new arrivals had brought with them from the States.

He checked his rearview mirror and made a mental note to keep an eye on the dark blue Jaguar sedan that pulled away at the same time. That car had not taken on any passengers, and Ripper was suspicious by nature.

Sir Jack Richardson, the government official seated next to Able Team in the rear, spoke in polished British tones. "Ripper, I want you to say hello to three gentlemen from America who are here to help us. Mr. Lyons, Mr. Blancanales and Mr. Schwarz have had the good fortune to procure through the auspices of a hotel key some information regarding the security of His Royal Highness, whose birthday is the day after tomorrow."

Richardson gave the men beside him a twinkling nod of appreciation. Able Team remained silent, looking ahead or at the scenes that passed the limousine's windows.

"It appears our friends here have gained access to the personal effects of the late John McElroy," the official continued. "Letters to Miss Kathleen McGowan, that blue-eyed bitch in NAL, indicate all is not well in our security. We have a continuing problem with Shillelagh. It's the sort of information, Ripper, that gets these American persons a special dispensation to bring ordnance into this country. Aren't you impressed?"

"Yeah, guv'nor," Ripper nodded. "It's a damn good thing they did." Looking into his mirror, he watched the blue Jag sink back into the medium to heavy traffic that trailed behind them on the three-lane highway connecting the airport with the capital.

Lyons noted Ripper's distraction and leaned forward.

"Get off at the next exit and find a nice quiet street," he said. He retrieved the three cases from the front seat.

Gadgets brought a pair of wire cutters to bear on the three seals and broke them. The warriors stripped off their suitcoats. Shoulder holsters for the Colt autopistols were strapped into place and the coats replaced. Ingram M-10s rested on their legs. Spare magazines for the weapons filled all jacket pockets.

Ripper pulled out his own piece, passed it back to Lyons and asked him to chamber a round. Sir Jack Richardson gazed at it. The weapon was a Beretta 93-R. The compact self-loading pistol was familiar to Able Team. Its fifteen 9mm missiles could be dispatched one at a time or in groups of three. But Able Team had abandoned the silenced version of this weapon. Carl was the first to make the switch to the modified Colt. His argument was that the silencer on the Beretta reduced the speed of the 115-grain bullets to subsonic. At that slow speed, a kill required a perfect headshot. Anything less would not necessarily stop the enemy, not the kind of enemy Able Team faced. The .45-caliber slugs of the Colt did considerably more damage at the slow speed required for a silenced weapon.

"This standard issue now?" Lyons asked Ripper.

"Not likely," the owner chuckled. Ripper was a convert to Mack Bolan's cause from years back, had been brought in on the Shillelagh case in recognition of his links with both the mob's lizardmen and Mack Bolan's global war, and now he looked with eager curiosity at the men who sat behind him.

Sir Jack Richardson produced an Uzi from a shelf beneath the seat. Standard issue for the Secret Service, the Israeli SMG could empty a 32-round magazine of 9mm flesh-shredders in just under three seconds. There were no Secret Servicemen in the car, nor in its proximity; the fear of personal sabotage had taken its toll and denied the American penetrators any protection. But the weapons of the Service remained in the car, primed and ready for use.

Ripper found the quiet street he was looking for and powered the limousine into a sharp turn. He brought the car to a halt immediately. Lyons and Schwarz jumped out and headed in opposite directions.

With the sound of the slammed doors, Ripper tromped the gas pedal and the car roared down the street. After about four hundred feet, he managed a controlled spin that brought it screeching across the street. It was still backing from its turn as Ripper and Richardson got out and ran for the buildings aft of the car. Blancanales had already exited and made for cover.

Ripper's "quiet street" was a fashionable residential row in the south London suburbs. It was lined with houses built close to the street. The side of one building nearly touched the side of its neighbor, leaving a narrow space between them.

The Jag took the corner very quickly. It flew past Lyons and Schwarz and headed toward the limousine. The driver stood on the brake. The big sedan's nose touched the side of the blocking vehicle. Four gunners clambered out brandishing AK-47s and Uzis. Two stayed with the Jag, while their partners went to the street corners and began a building-to-building sweep.

A Rover TC-3500 slowly turned the corner and came to a smooth stop at the top of the street. Four more men entered the scene. The new arrivals opened up.

Schwarz flattened as rounds chipped at the brickwork around his position. One chip grazed his right cheek below the eye. He inched forward, extending the muzzle of the Colt just past the edge of the wall, and a stroke of the trigger sent a three-round burst to the Rover. He jerked quickly back. He heard a dying man moaning as his life drained away into the London gutter.

Lyons directed another quick burst of persuaders toward the Rover. Targets died hurriedly.

The sweep began to fall apart. Colts dispatched 230-grain messages and brooked no reply. A string of crimson holes sprouted down the side of two enemy gunners as Ingram slugs stitched them from collar to crotch.

But Gadgets was still pinned down with a hail of 7.62mm lead. From fifty yards away, Ripper saw the American's predicament. The ex-mafioso gripped his weapon in two hands and sent three 9mm slugs to provide an edge in the confrontation. The slugs slammed into the shoulder and chest of the last visible gunner. Wounds gurgled as air leaked into the chest cavity.

Lyons looked around him. Residents remained cowering in their homes in the damp late afternoon. It was a scene that reminded him of Northern Ireland firefight footage he had studied back in the States. The air hung with palpable horror on all sides. Who knew where the next shot would come from?

Lyons took the risk. He ran to the nearest dying man. The guy looked up at him with fear and helplessness in his eyes. Lyons kicked him in the side.

The mortally wounded man groaned. "This ain't personal—I was just sent on a job...."

"And now?" Lyons glared at him, kneeling.

"Huh?"

"Now that I've wiped out your buddies, you still have no personal feelings about me?"

"Yeah. *No...!*"

The foresight of Lyons's Colt ripped along the guy's cheek, splitting the skin apart.

"Who sent you?" Lyons shouted.

The almost-dead tough found a last gasp of bravado.

"Fuck you! Wha'd you have to say to that?"

"That you're not a very interesting character," Lyons replied. Standing, he stroked the Colt's trigger with his forefinger.

ANY OTHER SURVIVORS from the Jag had split, presumably through the gaps between the buildings and away.

Ripper walked to the Rover and removed two of the bodies that lay in its path, leaving trails of red in his wake. He climbed into the Rover and was thankful that the keys to the car were still in the ignition. He didn't want to search the bodies. The car started smoothly and he moved it out of the way of the Secret

Service vehicle, feeling the bump as he drove over an arm. He parked, then returned to move the Jag away from the side of the limo.

Finally Ripper returned to sit at the wheel of the limo. He stared into the mirror at the men in the back seat, their bodies crouched next to the sweating figure of Sir Jack Richardson, their eyes darting about at all times.

What in the hell kind of men were these?

3

Settling back into the limo's front seat, Ripper took his passengers away from the battle-ground. The police were very efficient in London. The limo encountered a roadblock within two blocks. There had been no exterior damage to the car, and the diplomatic status of the vehicle guaranteed its passage through police lines without difficulty. The hardware rested snugly in the cases and the tinted windows of the vehicle prevented examination of its occupants.

Ripper drove on through wet streets to Grosvenor Square and the underground garage beneath the U.S. Embassy. There, Able Team went EVA in peace and quiet, disembarking and stretching their limbs and anxiously looking forward to some food and sleep. In the embassy itself, they were guided to quarters without introductions or interference. They had an hour or two before meeting with Leo.

Security for Leo Turrin had been a nightmare, so his arrivals and departures were secret and erratic. If the wrong people saw him in London, then eventually Leo could be assured of a slow and very painful death at the hands of a turkey doctor.

"Turkey" was a brutal form of torture, used by the mob to "interrogate" informants or to punish traitors. The victim's body was slowly brutalized until only a living mound of something resembling flesh remained. Throughout the ordeal, the victim was kept alive and fully aware of everything going on, screaming anything his torturers wanted to hear—anything to stop the pain.

Leo appeared at the embassy in the company of Sergeant Paul Henry, USMC. Sergeant Henry's expertise was survival under combat conditions. In Indochina, he'd earned a cluster of citations for bravery and resourcefulness. Before his London assignment he underwent a secret intensive training program taught by the U.S. Secret Service. The topic of that program was personal protection.

Henry called for an assembly of all those concerned in the Shillelagh matter and for the sleeping to be awakened. Within minutes, the three visiting American specialists caught their first sight in a long while of Stony Man buddy Leo Turrin. The men beamed recognition at each other.

Sergeant Henry presented himself to the small group of assembled staffers and visitors. "I was told that this was on a 'need-to-know' basis," he announced. "All I need to know is which of you gentlemen is Able Team."

The three warriors stepped forward and greeted Leo warmly, as others in the room began to talk amongst themselves, exchanging late-breaking information.

The four men were joined by the Marine sergeant as they went down to the garage to supervise the unloading of the weaponry. Leo watched Able Team open the trunk of the limo and reveal weapons of war provided by Sir Jack Richardson and the Secret Service. When Sergeant Henry saw the nature of the weaponry, he understood the scale of the coming war.

Three M-16/M-203s lay on top of the hoard. The M-16 was the battle-proven, standard-issue assault rifle for the U.S. armed forces. A breech-loaded grenade launcher, the M-203, was mounted under the M-16's barrel; 5.92mm ammo and 38mm high-explosive grenades made for a deadly combination.

Poking out between the fat rifles were radios, sheaths and webbing. Lyons delved into the smaller implements of war—HE and stun grenades, garrotes, additional magazines for the Colts and Ingrams, three Startron nightscopes. The battle ordnance was complete.

"How are you guys going to unpack this stuff and carry it around?" Leo asked. "Where am I supposed to get you a vehicle at this short notice?"

"How about right here," said Sergeant

Henry. He tossed a set of keys to Blancanales, along with the instructions: "A Ford Transit van is parked in Section B. It was mine. Now it's yours."

Pol left to locate the vehicle. Henry looked down at the arsenal stashed tightly in the huge trunk.

"I feel sorry for the bastards on the receiving end of this," he muttered.

"Don't waste your sympathy on them," Lyons said. "They deserve everything we're going to give them. What shape is the van in?"

"It's been modified in anticipation of your kind of needs," Henry said. "It's an RV that'll keep you alive, sir."

Gadgets drove the vehicle into view. The boxy van looked big enough to provide sleeping accommodations for four. Evident talents had been applied to a suspension system that was visible behind the wheels, and the engine cowling sported air-gulping cooling louvers. The vehicle looked prepared to hold its own against any of the leading British high- speed sedans. It had the additional quiet advantage of not bearing diplomatic plates, so the vehicle could blend in with Windsor's other tourist traffic.

The Americans spent the next half hour stowing the armament in the war wagon.

Then Leo spent time briefing Able Team on Windsor Castle. He mentioned a Mr. Geoffrey Hall, a former castle employee who would handle the final briefing. Hall was one of Brognola's contacts, and Leo wasn't too sure where the man fit in. The meeting would take place in a small pub in Windsor—the Boar and Bull.

Then Leo and Ripper spent hushed minutes going over the plans for a meeting later that day with one of Leo's contacts. The woman's name was Lady Carole Essex.

4

According to the file that Leo had secured from Stony Man Farm, Lady Carole, a cousin of the queen and thus in the line of royal succession, had since early childhood been interested in police work. It was not unusual for some of the royal cousins to hold jobs, and soon after she graduated, Lady Carole joined Scotland Yard. According to the record, Lady Carole had proven herself to be a diligent and capable worker, and soon became head clerk of the evidence vault at the New Scotland Yard headquarters. But after she'd been at the job for two years, a scandal broke. Drugs were finding their way out of the evidence vault and back into the streets.

When the drug ring was busted, Lady Carole too was convicted. As a felon, Lady Carole became the black sheep of the royal family. She had been dismissed from Scotland Yard, served time in prison and was still closely involved in the drug scene.

Since that first conviction, there had been a number of subsequent court appearances, mostly relating to drug trafficking. For the past several months, she was known to be involved with John McElroy's bunch.

Leo was aware that the scandal in the evidence vault was true for the most part. But what was not in the official files was the fact that Lady Carole had been approached by the ringleaders after working in the vault for about six months. She reported the contact to her superiors, who decided to set up a "sting operation" in order to bring down the ring. Lady Carole was an integral part of the sting, and for eighteen months the lady played her part to perfection, arranging for the drugs to go out of the vault and altering the records accordingly.

She wore a body pack to several meetings. The recordings were used to set up situations in which the ringleaders could be caught with their fingers dirty. She found the work exciting, and she developed a talent for undercover work. In order to preserve her value as an undercover agent, it was arranged for her to be convicted of various crimes in connection with the operation.

With her cover intact, the lady had proved to be very effective in subsequent operations. She had been doing this for about five years when she made it into McElroy's circle.

It had been Lady Carole who tipped off Leo Turrin to the *Canal Queen*. But he had never met her, had only communicated with her through Sir Jack Richardson.

Now Leo very much wanted to find out what the lady knew about Shillelagh.

He closed his eyes in thought as the limo weaved through London traffic to the meeting.

Leo had found Lady Carole to be an excellent pipeline into the NAL. Besides being one of his operation's most reliable couriers, she was McElroy's lover.

Now the operation was broken, but new heat was coming down. Apparently Leo's work in fingering the Manhattan dope transfer, then bringing specialists into London, was stirring things up.

The word was out, of course, about the specialists. Subversion was winning the war for now. But the chain that led to Shillelagh was shorter all the time—damn short, in fact. The attack on Sir Jack's limousine was obviously intended to be a sudden and complete wipeout.

Leo knew that more blood would flow very soon as the specialists did their job.

This morning's meeting was to take place at the Tower of London. Leo Turrin's mind drifted back to the last time he'd met someone at the Tower.

It was early in the Executioner's war against the Mafia. Bolan had found himself in England, trying to get home after the battles in France.

In their efforts to bring an end to the "Bolan problem," the mob chieftains had mounted a two-pronged attack against Mack. One prong was the war party led by Arnie "The Farmer" Castiglione. The other prong was the peace party sent to offer Bolan employment in the mob.

Leo, in his undercover role as mobster, was part of the peace party and a meeting between Leo and Mack took place in the Tower—appropriately on Execution Row. In the aftermath of that meeting, Arnie was given his ticket to hell by Mack Bolan.

As the limo pulled to a smooth stop on Tower Hill, Leo opened his eyes to the present. He was accompanied in the car by his personal bodyguard, Sergeant Henry, who sat beside him, and Ripper Dan Aliotto, hit man turned chauffeur for the truth-and-justice team, who drove. Leo Turrin was swathed in bandages.

He would stay in the car, guarded by Sergeant Henry, while Ripper made the rendezvous with the lady in the Tower. If she was amenable to Ripper's suggestion, they would return to the car and the four would simply drive around. Once Leo and Lady Carole were finished, she would be returned to the Tower.

Ripper and Henry got out of the car. Ripper headed off to meet the lady. Henry held his Uzi at the ready under a folded raincoat.

After ten minutes, Ripper returned with a petite blonde. Leo took a good look at the lady and enjoyed the rest his tired eyes were getting. She was tiny—about five one—and beautiful. Her hair fell in gentle waves about her shoulders, and even behind large dark glasses the fine cheekbones were apparent. The coat she wore almost hid the curves, but not quite.

Ripper opened the back door of the car and she climbed in. Leo stared at her. The car pulled away from the curb.

The woman settled into the seat. She removed the dark glasses and opened the coat. The promise was fulfilled; soft curves pressed against a white blouse, and her skirt rose inches up shapely thighs as she sat back in the plush upholstery. His eyes drifted up toward her face and Leo found himself staring into a lovely smile, eyes and lips sparkling in greeting. She was quite aware of the effect she was having on the man in the bandages.

"You look like the 'Invisible Man,' Mr. Sticker," she said, then laughed. Leo joined in the laughter as well as he could, his smile visible between the strips of bandages.

"It may look ridiculous, but it keeps me alive," he said.

One hour later, the limo returned to the Tower. Sergeant Henry got out and opened the rear door as Leo sighed with genuine regret. He hadn't been able to speak entirely freely to this woman, but they both sensed the bond beginning between them.

The blonde beauty walked briskly back to the Tower and joined a crowd of tourists. Sergeant Paul Henry scanned the area to ensure that no one was paying undue attention to her.

The Marine's head snapped back. The impact of the bullet sprayed the limo with blood.

Before Leo and Ripper could react to the

loss of their only guard, the back door flew open and a man jumped into the car, the muzzle of his Uzi pointing directly at Leo's swathed head. The front passenger door opened and a second man joined them. Leo packed a Colt Python—but the first man had expertly searched the Fed and come away with it.

The second man ordered Ripper to roll. Ripper's fist, held in an iron grip by his captor, contained both keys and Colt in clumsy disorder; he was soon disarmed. Leo cursed. He and Ripper had been forced to make this meet with small numbers—no heavy armament, no backup for a secret meeting with a double agent in the royal family. That was the way it had to be, and it had backfired.

One of the assailants pulled a folded canvas sack from under his jacket and placed it over Leo's head. The same man gave Ripper directions, leaning over the partition that separated the driver's compartment from the rear passenger area. His partner sat in front, silent, pointing a semiautomatic at Ripper's groin. After twenty minutes of following directions, Ripper parked on command.

The back door of the limo opened and Leo was pulled out onto the sidewalk.

Ripper never heard the report of the gun as it boomed within the close confines of the car, nor did he feel the impact of the bullet as it parted bone and brain on its way through his skull. The bullet emerged to continue through the windshield of the car, leaving a star-shaped, blood-soaked glass memorial to an Able Team ally who did his duty because of a burning conviction that it was right.

The murderer quickly got out of the limo and ran to a Ford Granada parked behind them. Leo and his abductor were already in the back seat. The bandaged, trussed and bagged Leo fought with the man on hearing the gunshot that ended Ripper's life. The man viciously clubbed his struggling captive. Ripper's killer settled into the driver's seat and tore off, tires smoking.

LEO HAD NO IDEA HOW LONG he was unconscious, but he came to in a room with cement walls, an overhead light, and the chair he sat in. Ropes bound him hand and foot. The bandages that had hidden his identity had been removed. He was stripped to the waist. On his chest he felt small electrodes. Leo knew what these were for and knew that his situation was desperate.

"Good to see you awake, Mr. Sticker." The voice came at Leo from all sides. It was a deep mechanical voice, not unlike the synthesized voice in electronic toys. Leo noticed the television camera for the first time. It was in a corner of the room and took in the full sweep of Leo's prison.

"You have been looking for me for quite some time," the electronic voice droned, "and now you have found me. I am Shillelagh. You will get to know me rather well over the next little while, but I don't think the experience will be pleasant for either of us. I am a professional, Mr. Sticker, and I *will* do what is necessary. From the little I know about you, I suspect that there could be great profit in knowing more about you. A mixture of drugs and other, shall we say, physical inducements should prove effective in obtaining all of the information I need. Shall we begin?''

Leo writhed in pain as a ball of electricity hit him, dispersed like SMG slugs ripping into his marrow. The current was reduced until it became a steady throb, tolerable but insistent. From somewhere behind, Leo heard a door open and a person walk in.

Moisture was applied to his bicep. He felt a needle pierce his skin. The sound of hard-soled shoes on the cement floor followed the needle out of the room. The current was switched off. As the drug took effect, Leo felt himself drifting into a moonless night that beckoned him like a lover. I'm ready, baby, he thought helplessly. I am ready.

The voice began asking the questions. Probing, insisting, all powerful. An evasion or wrong answer brought Leo to screams as the shock was applied. Then Leo was allowed to drift back again under the drug's influence before the voice resumed its interrogation.

5

The war wagon cruised south along the A332 highway into Windsor.

The castle had been in view for some five minutes. It loomed above the fertile green countryside like a gray sentinel. Built on top of Castle Hill, the royal "weekend retreat" was surrounded by a stone wall that stretched for more than five hundred feet in a radius around the imposing Round Tower.

The minute they saw it, the castle distracted Able Team from the task of cleaning personal weaponry for the upcoming night work. The three warriors stared at the structure, trying to fit what they saw into the detailed picture given them that morning by Leo.

Leo had described the historic building in terms of its sections.

The western section, called the Lower Ward, is an open-ended courtyard, surrounded on the three closed sides by the castle walls. Integrated into the structure of the walls themselves is a large chapel and associated buildings, and quarters for the castle guards. Towers project from the walls at regular intervals.

The Middle Ward is a large grass-covered mound. On top of it sits the bulky Round Tower.

The east boundary of the Middle Ward is a wall that by the standards of this castle is thin—about a foot and a half. At the north end of the wall, a gate leads into the Upper Ward beyond.

As in the Lower Ward, the walls of the Upper Ward have sprouted extensions into the center courtyard, and rooms and quarters of all kinds have been built within these stone extensions.

It was here that the State Apartments began, filling what was once called King Charles II House. This was originally the residence of the royal family itself, who are now housed in the nearby George IV House. The two residences were cozy nests indeed, but not immune to vermin.

Blancanales pulled the van into a parking lot in Peascod Street, across from the Lower Ward. Able Team joined tourists who had been turned back from the castle and sat puzzled in their cars, wondering whether to wait out the closure of the attractions associated with the castle that were scattered along its walls. But Lyons, Blancanales and Schwarz studied the stately architecture for weaknesses in the castle's defenses.

Despite intense pressure in Washington to pull Able Team out of its recent Central American mission, it was in fact Able Team's own urgent sympathy for Leo Turrin's position in

London that had brought them to this new arena. The three warriors of Able Team were justice-hungry, ready to reach for victory in this new People's War.

Their trained eyes picked out the SAS snipers on the roof of both King George IV House and King Charles II House. The barrels of the L42A1's were clearly visible. This was a British hard set, and it troubled Able Team. They knew the British had a "by the book" approach to the horrors of terrorism, and Lyons had been told more than once of the British propensity for using geegaws such as the QuickPoint. Big deal. A device like the Quick-Point sniperscope summed up the likely flaws in the defenses of the castle they had come to protect. The trick with the QuickPoint scope was to get the red dot to follow the bouncing target. QuickPoint was nothing special for a good rifleman. Lyons appreciated it had some application in law enforcement, since the red dot served as a warning to a suspect or escaping prisoner. "See the red dot? That's where the bullet will hit." But the red dot did not illuminate the target, it did not identify the target; it identified the point of impact, whether it was a head, a tree, a leaf. It did not aid in accuracy, as the rifle could still waver. In fact it betrayed the rifleman. The target saw the red dot, dodged fast, fired at the QuickPoint scope. Dead rifleman.

The three American specialists stepped from

the van and mingled with the tourists. Their casual English sportswear disguised their true background.

They stopped a pedestrian and asked for directions. Within minutes they found themselves at the inn called the Boar and Bull.

The tavern occupied the ground floor of an ancient house on Clarence Street, away from the castle. Unlike the public houses selling drinks on High Street, the Boar and Bull was a local—it catered to the citizenry of the town. Tourists went elsewhere.

The odor of hot steak pies assailed the warriors as they entered. A tall man of about seventy, with a thick white mustache that curled at the ends, immediately approached them. He introduced himself as Geoffrey Hall.

Carl Lyons did not introduce himself or the other two. He openly studied the man.

Hall was a shade taller than six feet, and slender. His bearing had the stamp of the British military. He wore a navy blue double-breasted blazer with a crest on the chest pocket, and gray flannel slacks. Strength radiated from the old man. His eyes impressed Lyons. They spoke of much life lived and more yet to come. They proclaimed it worthwhile to carry on, even in the valley of the shadow of death.

"You gentlemen will find the food here to be very good. May I recommend the shepherd's pie?" The elegant ex-soldier led the three specialists to a corner table that held a half-empty pint of very dark beer.

"I should caution you that our beer is much stronger than what you are used to in America," the old man added.

"I'll drink what you're drinking," Lyons said.

A barmaid took their order. Conversation of an inconsequential nature occupied the four men until food and drink arrived. As they ate, the specialists found out more about their host.

During World War II, Geoffrey Hall had served with the OSS as an agent behind enemy lines in occupied France. His mother was French, and he spoke the language like a native. He also had a supply sergeant's talent for organization and acquisition—a talent that was put to good use in setting up and equipping several units of the French Resistance. More than once he organized raids that equipped the freedom fighters with weapons from German arsenals.

After the war, he applied for service in the Royal Household Staff Corps. He was quickly accepted, and within a few years his organizational and acquisitional talents were utilized as Chief of Household Services, Windsor Castle. He retired from the position five years earlier.

During Stony Man's research into Leo's Shillelagh mission, Hall's name had emerged as the best source of information on the inner workings of Windsor Castle. Now he briefed Able Team on every room and corridor of each strategic zone in the castle. The briefing was lengthy, punctuated by moments taken to sketch key elevations on a scrap of paper. Distilling and absorbing the information was a trial of memory for the three visitors.

"The prince's birthday dinner will be held in the Waterloo Chamber," the crusty Briton said in closing. "The dining table accommodates one hundred fifty people, although tonight's dinner will be a little smaller—about one hundred twenty."

"A small, intimate, family dinner," Lyons volunteered. He wiped froth and a sour grin from his jaw with a backhanded gesture. "Maybe we should join them."

6

The rear door of the war wagon swung open at seven-thirty-three that evening, and three shadowy figures joined the descending night. Their weapons they carried openly. They wore black nightsuits with black watch caps covering their heads.

The contents of the war wagon were distributed among the three men. Each carried an M-16/M-203, a suppressed M-10 on a strap, and a silenced Colt in a hip holster. Radios hung on the opposite side of the belts to the Colts. Grenades and extra magazines were touch-placed on the bandoliers. A Startron nightscope hung on the webbing of each nightsuit.

Politician and Lyons carried two garrotes each. Coiled around Lyons's left shoulder, safely out of the way of the weapons of war, was a rope.

The three men moved to their positions.

Gadgets headed south along High Street, moving from house to house. When he reached the intersection of Park Street, he turned east and worked his way through narrow cobbled

streets to the edge of Home Park and the south
front of the castle. A door opened and spilled
light onto the street. Two couples came out of
the house. They saw the heavily armed man
and all conversation stopped. Gadgets nodded,
continued walking at a measured pace. The
success of his cool was confirmed by snatches
of the resumed conversation behind him. The
couples merely commented on the fortresslike
atmosphere of Windsor, not admitting to their
fright.

Gadgets reached the border of Home Park
and melted into the rows of trees at the west
side of the Long Walk. Between him and the
castle wall ran an iron fence. With his radio he
sent a signal to his partners that he was in position. He ensured he was fully covered by the
trees. At any moment he could be picked off
by an alert sniper on the castle roof.

Lyons and Blancanales carefully explored
Thames Street, which ran beneath the North
Terrace. They found the street had been
blocked off, two bobbies manning a barrier.
The policemen were covered by snipers on the
roofs of houses overlooking the street.

Like wraiths, Lyons and Blancanales backed
away. Their new objective was the One Hundred Steps.

Built in a previous age, the One Hundred
Steps led from the town to the castle's North
Terrace. The stone stairs, worn down from
centuries of use, were flanked by low stone

bannisters. The gateway barring access to the steps was guarded by two British troopers in full combat gear, toting standard British issue Sterling SMGs that spewed five hundred fifty 9mm rounds per minute.

Blancanales found cover in the deep shadows of an evergreen near parked cars, some distance away from the steps. Here he would wait. He sent a two-click signal to Gadgets and felt the tap on his shoulder that marked the departure of Lyons.

As the Ironman moved off, Pol sent a silent prayer into the night. When the two men first met, Carl was an L.A. cop, a good one. Then Lyons became a true soldier—one of the hardest soldiers that Pol had ever known. Lyons was now a legend. But the current situation presented a special challenge. Able Team knew something bad was about to happen and they would move to stop it, but they could not expect back-up of any sort because acknowledgement of their existence might tip a traitor. At best it would tip off British intelligence that there indeed was a traitor among them. Either way the lid would blow too soon.

They had to do it their way, Able Team's way, and that meant Lyons, true to character, would have to go up the wall.

LYONS WORKED HIS WAY along the shadows of tree-lined Thames Street toward the east end of the castle. He knew that an encounter would prove disastrous. These were friendly forces, and he could not fire back.

Soon Thames Street followed the curve between the castle wall and a small section of woodland. Lyons found a hiding place between bushes growing beneath a stand of linden trees.

He looked at the stone wall. It was not immense. It protected only the outer limits of this part of the castle, which held parkland and a forest as small but as dense as the woodland on the outside. He could see the tops of elm trees swaying within the grounds.

From the top of the wall jutted metal spikes to deter trespassers.

Lyons crouched deep in the shadows. He unwound the rope and tied a small loop at one end. He peered out from his position.

He jerked back as two British sentries approached in the night. He watched them pass, holding himself rigid and unbreathing. Their uniforms told him they were Welsh Guardsmen.

They chatted amiably on their patrol, ignorant of what lurked to one side. Lyons watched them. Terrorist atrocities occurred with mounting regularity in Britain, but nothing had yet shaken the islanders' native sangfroid and resigned tolerance. Naked fear was not known in Britain to the degree it was elsewhere.

As the sentries' sauntered paces faded into the night, Lyons waited for minutes more, then made his move.

The rope caught on the first toss. Silently he scrambled up. Exposed at the top for perilous seconds against the night sky, Lyons unhitched the rope from the spike and carried it with him as he jumped down into the bushes on the other side. He absorbed the impact of his drop on bended knees, ending in the right-shoulder roll that Bolan taught him. He came up short behind the sheltering trunk of an elm.

His M-16/M-203 swung automatically into position as he sighted the glowing end of a cigarette at head-height in the shadow of a tree fifty yards away. "Beejaysus, dat's good stuff," the shadow said to itself. Lyons's motor revved on recognition of the accent. Contact confirmed.

The ember continued to glow, periodically burning brighter as the Irishman toked noisily on his prebattle spliff. Battle hash was a common custom in Nam, but Lyons was surprised to see an Irishman smoking up before combat. Welcome to the eighties.

Lyons stripped himself of his combat gear and pulled a Bowie knife from its sheath on his thigh. Silence was imperative, and the Bowie fit that criterion. He moved out on his belly. The orange ember glowed brighter in the otherwise black night. The smoker sucked a hearty lungful. "Christmas, dat's good," the voice said to no one.

Lyons crawled in a semicircle toward his target. When the ember glowed brightly again, he raised himself into a crouch, ran noiselessly to-

ward the target. He staggered the pot smoker
with an open-handed blow to the forehead.
Then he dragged the knife blade backhand
across the man's carotid and jugular. It was an
effortless kill.

The joint burned in the grass beside the
corpse. Lyons ground it out with the toe of his
Israeli combat boot. He heard more Irish
voices calling hoarsely into the velvet night.

"Micky, ya' dere?"

"Micky lad, where is ya'?"

Lyons's heart skipped a beat. His grenade
launcher and other fighting gear were fifty
yards behind him. He would have to dispose of
both terrorists, using his wits and the knife.

The pointman passed within inches of his
position. Lyons could not see him but he felt
the air move as he passed, and he smelled the
odor of tobacco on the guy's clothes. With pa-
tience and professionalism learned from Blancanales, Lyons waited for the second man. The
moon broke briefly through a cloud.

He saw a heavily armed figure walking
through the trees. "He'll be spliffin' da'
weed," the man said. "See if it ain't true."
Lyons came on him in the dark. He reached
around the man's head with his left hand and
clapped the mouth shut. With his right hand,
he drove the Bowie knife deep under the
breastbone. Both men fell together to the
forest floor.

"Ya' may be right, Stevie," the first man

answered, "but we still need the bastard. Right?"

"Uh-huh," said Lyons in the dark. The terrorist's talk had given him a good fix on the guy.

With a smooth, practiced motion, he flung the bloody blade into the middle of the voice.

"I'm kill't!" gurgled the terrorist.

"Good t'ing, too," muttered Lyons.

WHATEVER ELSE HE THOUGHT of that Kathleen McGowan bitch, Michael O'Shea had to admit she was one hell of an organizer. During the past two months, thirty-five people involved in the night's operation had undergone training in both Northern Ireland and England, and their leaders had visited the castle as tourists and had studied its interior plans under McGowan's careful eye.

O'Shea knew the information and training would serve him well.

His group was to secure the west end of the North Terrace. O'Shea and his four men had scaled the wall some distance west of the One Hundred Steps, using the trees as cover. The killers with O'Shea carried AK-47s and two HE grenades each. O'Shea held a silenced Uzi; the advantage of silence for the night's work outweighed the loss of accuracy incurred by the silencer.

O'Shea checked his watch, shielding the digital timepiece with his hand so its glow would not give them away. Timing was essential; if he moved earlier than 8:30, his group's actions would not be coordinated with those of the other two assault teams and the attack would fail.

Moments before 8:30, a five-man British patrol slowly made its way down the One Hundred Steps, looking for anything out of place in the forest on both sides of the worn steps. O'Shea heard the thud of the combat boots on the stone. He waited patiently for the first casualties of the night.

The patrol leader had no time to warn his companions. The 9mm parabellums from O'Shea's Uzi tore into his throat. The remainder of the patrol died quickly as the silent onslaught continued. The clatter of their weapons on stone was the only signal that something was amiss.

Two sentries in the street below heard the clatter. Quickly they opened the gate at the bottom of the steps and headed up them toward the noise. So intent were they on their objective that neither noticed the black-clad man slip out of the shadows and follow them. Once through the gate, Blancanales vaulted the left bannister of the steps and followed the two men as they climbed. While moving, Pol transmitted a pair of double clicks, advising his partners that the battle was on.

O'Shea's finger stroked the trigger of the Uzi again as the two British sentries came up the steps. One of the troopers slipped in the rivulets of blood that washed down the center of the worn stone. Before he could recover, his own life ran out to join with the crimson stream. A heartbeat later, his companion fell. Stillness returned to the night as the stream flowed on.

From experience gained in the jungles of Nam, Blancanales knew the art of moving silently through a forest. Among the elms and sycamores of this English hill, he was in his element. When he saw the brief flashes from the Uzi, he hurled himself up off the steps and into the undergrowth. He wriggled into hiding. He pulled the Startron from his nightsuit webbing.

Five men were silhouetted in the night-scope's eerie light.

As more boots thudded on the steps, Blancanales saw the five Irishmen move farther into the shadows to strike again. Stealthily he unlimbered his Colt.

CORPORAL PHILLIPS had become concerned when the five-man patrol did not radio in. The route down the One Hundred Steps had been timed during the drills, and they should have radioed Phillips from the bottom of the steps two minutes earlier.

Phillips advised his CO of the problem and, with Private Scott, headed down to check on the missing patrol.

The two men reacted immediately as they

came within sight of the corpses, but immediately was not fast enough, and Private Scott died where he fell.

As O'Shea swung his Uzi around to take out Phillips, two .45-caliber slugs from Blancanales's Colt found the terrorist's head. O'Shea's finger tightened on the Uzi trigger, sending random blasts of 9mm slugs into the night. The slugs found one of O'Shea's fellow terrorists, dispatching him with silent holes.

A second burst from the Colt sent another ambusher to join O'Shea.

Phillips had ducked when Scott fell. Now he raised his head. The muzzle of his L2A3 hovered just in front of his chin.

He saw two shadows moving. He stood up, aimed at one of them, fired, saw the other one crumple, then the first one, too, before he ducked back down.

Silence descended. Phillips slowly raised his head again. He knew he had an ally in the night.

Holding his Sterling level, the young corporal moved slowly down the steps until a whispered voice from the forest on his right stopped him.

"Friend," said the voice.

Blancanales emerged from the shadows and joined the British soldier. Quickly the American filled him in on the revised picture.

At the top of the steps, a voice from Phillips's radio demanded explanations.

FROM THEIR NATURAL BLIND IN THE TREES the roof of the castle was just over two hundred fifty yards away—nearly point-blank range for their Russian rifles. Collins and Donegal scanned the top of the east wall. Four orange blobs glowed along the roof. British snipers' sites.

They heard the sound of the SMG far off to their right. O'Shea was having problems. It was time to go to work.

Almost as one, the two terrorists fired. A millisecond later, two of the orange blobs dissolved.

Carl Lyons, M-16 cradled in his arms, crouched just below the east end of the Sunken Garden. The reports of the two weapons to his left signaled the start of the battle in his sector. He began to crawl toward the source of the sounds.

The two snipers fired again. Lyons caught a hint of movement in the trees to his left.

He loaded an HE grenade into the 203, and with a pump, shot it into the middle of three flank men who had appeared in the darkness, black on black. The steel fragments propelled by thirty-five grams of explosive tore into the Irishmen. Screams cut through the night like an animal's cries. The roar of the M-16 restored silence to the scene.

Then two more booming reports. Lyons rolled to the cover of the trees.

FOUR RIFLEMEN ON THE EAST ROOF lay dead, shards from their nightscopes buried in what was left of their faces.

One of the snipers from the north roof moved to take their place. The British sniper was quickly joined by another, and the two men trained their scopes along the trees at the leading edge of the forest.

A light squeeze on the trigger by one of them and the shadow of a terrorist disappeared into the trees.

The second sniper tracked onto Donegal. The 7.62 NATO round thwacked into the back of the terrorist's head, exploding in a crimson spray of teeth and bone as it exited through the mouth.

Collins turned to see his partner's head explode, then dived for cover as a second round from the L42A1 chopped into a tree.

Collins brought the SVD around. A sigh, a squeeze, and a 7.62mm whoosh of death was dispatched to the castle roof. He rode the recoil and pulled once more.

He was not able to pull a third time; a NATO round had shattered his spine.

JOSEPH FLYNN's squad number three worked through the forest by the eastern edge of the Sunken Garden. One man was walking point, followed closely by Flynn and two other men.

Lyons had a hot reception ready for the four of them. The M-16 sent a full load into the pointman. Flynn and the two surviving terrorists dived for cover in the trees.

Flynn fired his Uzi at the source of the shots.

Another blast from the M-16 took out one of his companions.

Flynn and the survivor, Kelly, continued toward their objective, the steps that led up the far end of the Sunken Garden.

Flynn kept up a stream of covering fire as Kelly headed for the steps with his only LAW. Pausing just long enough to change the Uzi's magazines, Flynn kept Lyons pinned. Kelly made the stairs leading to the top of the Sunken Garden.

Kelly extended the tube of the LAW, readying it for use against an advancing group of British soldiers.

With a whoosh, the antipersonnel rocket blasted into the middle of the little knot.

Shrapnel cut into the men like a hail of meat cleavers. Cleanly severed parts of human beings littered the air. Kelly threw the now useless tube away and unslung his AK-47. Scrambling up the steps, he ran onto the south side of the terrace and began a zigzag dash to the doors of the State Apartments.

Lyons, firing bursts at Flynn's position, moved out of the forest in pursuit of Kelly.

Lyons raced up the stairs, halted and raised his rifle. He took careful aim and fired a blast of 5.56 rounds at the running figure. Kelly's zag became a tumble as a 55-grain slug caught him in the back and pushed him over the wall.

Flynn was now dashing toward the doors

that would take him into the Apartments. As he ran he hurled a grenade at the doorway.

The explosion blasted the doors open, and the terrorist ran through.

FROM HIS POSITION in the sheltering trees at the western edge of Home Park, Gadgets heard the whine of high-powered engines coming toward him. He turned to look, saw three Land Rovers racing along Park Street.

He held up his Startron and took a closer look at the vehicles. In the cab of each Land Rover rode two men. The backs of the vehicles were covered with tarpaulins that might be concealing other men.

If they were reinforcements for the beleaguered British snipers, they were welcome. If not, they were dire trouble.

Telling friend from foe in a firefight can be hard, and an error had terrible consequences. In Able Team's war, the problem was paramount. Their fight was directed only at legitimate targets, terrorists and those who actively supported the pattern of death that followed terrorists wherever they went. If Bolan's men fired without knowing *for certain* that their target was a legitimate one, then they became no different than the murdering terrorists. Gadgets fretted over each second of delay while the new players in the deadly game remained unknown.

The three vehicles reached the castle's gate.

The lead vehicle rammed the gate, tearing it from its ancient hinges. The ornamental iron-work hardly slowed the vehicle. It raced through the opening, taking tangled metal with it, followed by the other two Land Rovers.

As the three vehicles accelerated up the long walk, a blast from an LAW in the lead vehicle opened the next obstacle, the King George IV Gate, in a flurry of smoke and debris.

The last vehicle to enter the inner gate received a 40mm grenade from Gadgets's M-203. From his position on the slope above the walk, Gadgets saw the grenade land on the tarp and explode with a dull whump. He fired a second grenade and the vehicle burst into a ball of flame, a funeral pyre for the two men in front and any others concealed beneath the tar-paulin.

British soldiers poured from the Norman Gate in pursuit of the other two vehicles. A second LAW collapsed the Norman Gate's overhanging stone, crushing several soldiers underneath.

Automatic-rifle fire from within the Land Rovers cut through the survivors like a scythe.

7

Her Majesty had arrived at Windsor Castle shortly before six o'clock.

Dinner was served promptly at eight. One hundred twenty-seven guests had filed into the Waterloo Chamber.

They were just finishing the first course when they heard the opening shots in the battle.

Within seconds, eleven soldiers barged into the dining room. Their leader ran to Sergeant Stephen Mallik, Her Majesty's personal bodyguard.

At one time, Mallik and the queen had had a stormy relationship. Security for the British sovereign was always a touchy issue because the royal family refused to live as prisoners. Gradually the relationship between the bodyguard and his charge evolved into mutual respect. Security remained tight—tighter than Her Majesty cared for—but not oppressively so.

Mallik and the other troops began to herd the assembled guests under the huge polished oak table.

Without protest, the queen, too, ducked under the table.

Mallik and the soldiers piled up chairs to form a barricade. It would not give much protection, but it was better than nothing.

Mallik stayed close to the queen. Together they heard the explosions and they heard the sound of men dying to protect the royal family.

Beneath the table, each individual tried to deal with the possibility of impending death. More than a few began to weep.

A child near the queen was crying. The monarch pulled the frightened little girl to her and tried to offer her comfort.

Mallik frantically removed his suitcoat and tie to give greater freedom of movement.

Soldiers dressed in camouflage combat fatigues aimed Sterlings or L1A1s at the six entrances to the room. The L1A1 was a powerful, dependable weapon that had seen service from the jungles of the Far East to the windswept Falklands.

An explosion blew the east door off its hinges.

Pieces of wood flew through the air, some absorbed by the cushions of the upturned chairs. One of the splinters caught a soldier in the right eye; he was dead before he hit the floor.

A second soldier fell to the fusillade of parabellums streaming into the room through the open doorway.

A low moaning came from beneath the table. Several slugs had torn through the barricade of chairs, finding human flesh.

Flynn slammed a fresh magazine into his Uzi, then dived. He issued a challenge of fire, finding the soldier at the southeast corner of the room. The 9mm slugs punched into the man, standing him straight up before dropping him to the floor.

Flynn rolled quickly, knowing that if he stopped even for a second he would be dead. He instinctively fired another burst from the Uzi. An advancing soldier caught the bullets in the face and throat. Blood sprayed out of the severed jugular, splattering the walls with splotches of red. The flow continued unabated onto the rug around the collapsed body.

Now the southwest corner door blew inward, propelled by an HE grenade. Mallik shielded his face from splinters, but there was no shelter from the 7.62 missiles that followed. His arms fell away from a bloodied face as he died on the floor.

A terrorist dived into the room through the newly blown door. Though he came in low, slugs from an L1A1 caught him in middive. He landed in a crumpled heap.

A grenade bounced into the room from the same entrance. Lance Corporal Andrew Hollinger would earn a posthumous Victoria Cross for covering the explosive with his body in a fine low racing dive. Now a crimson puddle spread out from Andrew's torso where it lay grotesquely askew.

Two terrorists came in firing. One walked high and was thrown against the west wall by 7.62 slugs from the L1A1s. The one who crouched low had more success, his AK rounds finding soldiers who tumbled against each other, propping each other up momentarily before they all slumped into a heap on the floor.

Flynn crawled around the head of the table and opened up. His fire thwacked into the walls.

A terrorist had made it to the edge of the table near the queen and was advancing under Flynn's cover.

He stopped and pulled back a chair. A British soldier poked his head out of the space. The terrorist fired a short burst at it, turning it to bloody pulp.

The killer bellowed out, "Any one else makes a move and the queen is dead. I want all weapons on the floor."

Recognizing that further action would be fatal to the royal family, the remaining British soldiers put down their weapons. More terrorists entered the room. One of them was terrorist mastermind Kathleen McGowan. She opened up her Uzi on the unarmed soldiers, dropping each man like a pot of hot noodles hurled into a sieve to drain.

Quiet fell upon the room in a pall, disturbed only by the moaning of the injured and the soft crying of the children.

Two terrorists began picking up weapons. The terrorist at the edge of the table did not move his AK from its target, the queen.

Kathleen took a quick look around the room at her victory.

With these hostages, she and her people would be able to walk right out of the castle.

8

She grew uneasy as the first flush of victory wore off. She had not expected to achieve it without losses, but the losses had been high indeed.

Of the three squads attacking the north side, only Flynn had survived—and judging by his shotgun wounds, he might not yet.

Seven of the main force from the Land Rovers were dead. A graze on her shoulder reminded Kathleen of just how close she had come to joining them.

When the attack against the castle had first been proposed by Shillelagh several months ago, Kathleen thought the idea preposterous. With Shillelagh's help, she turned a preposterous idea into a workable plan. The plan had been launched and the raid had succeeded.

The next step was to get out.

Kathleen pulled a list from her pocket. Shillelagh had provided the names of each member of the royal family and photograph for each name on the list. Thirty-five people.

Each corpse in the room was examined—eliminating four of the names on the list. As terrorists herded the family out from under the table, each face was scanned.

Kathleen separated the hostages into two groups. The first was made up of the survivors on the list, the second were those not on the list. The second group could be let go; it was the first group that mattered. Kathleen went up to an old man who was being set free and handed him the sheet of names and photographs. She gave her instructions in a soft Irish brogue. "When you and the others in your group leave this room, give the list to whoever is in charge out there. The people on the list will be released on payment of one million pounds sterling, in a manner that the authorities will be told of shortly.

"If anyone attempts to follow us when we leave, we will immediately kill the hostages. If our demands are not met, we will begin killing individual hostages starting with the last name on the list and working toward the first.

"Within fifteen minutes, I want a bus brought out to the front of the castle. One of my people will go and check it out. No harm must come to him, or some of these people die."

THE TWENTY-FOURTH EARL OF KINTAIL was not the best man Kathleen might have picked for the task. The tall, clear-eyed gentleman from Northern Ireland had an iron will and a sense of duty to the royal family that went beyond mere patriotism.

The earl was a bastard. As an only child, his legal right to his father's title had fallen in a muddy area of British common law, and the courts had decided against him. Over forty years ago the crestfallen young man had learned of the court's decision against him in his digs in London.

In the short span of a few hours his entire life had changed. In the rigidly structured British army of the thirties, he could never hope to achieve a prominent place without the edge his title had given him. By withdrawing his title, the courts had condemned him to a middle-echelon position where his fine training and talents would be frustrated. He was an eager young man then, with a young man's ambitions.

The courts had also made him ashamed of his parents, something that, until then, Eddie had thought impossible. At school and at university, he had never endured the insults of his fellows. He remembered how the biggest boy in All Saints had called him a "shrewd little bastard" in front of his class. He heard the snickering around him and turned to face the rest of the boys. "I am a *royal* bastard," he said in his loudest and most precise voice. Then he broke the bully's nose.

Such moments became a source of strength for Eddie, but the news of the court's decision had made his pride disappear. He felt as he had felt as a child holding a fistful of hail pellets tightly in his hands; he remembered his disappointment as the perfect white pearls melted and dripped through his closed fingers.

"Hello Eddie," the voice had said more than forty years ago. "No lad, don't get up." Eddie had not seen the King of England since his father's funeral, but the man now stood inside the doorway of his London apartment. "I heard the news. Bad luck, Eddie, old boy. I expect you'd like to get drunk, what? Do you have any brandy?"

While sipping the liquor, the king explained that under British law, Eddie's father's estate would become the property of the British crown. In effect, the king could do anything he liked with all of the Kintail estate.

"Did you know, Eddie," the king asked, "that there have been Kintails in the House of Lords since the days of that upstart Cromwell?" The king smiled. "Of course you did," he continued. "So I think it would be a damn shame to lose a family that has been such a bear for punishment for such a long time. What I mean to say, Eddie, is that there have been Kintails in our service since the time before the Empire.

"Are you married, Eddie? No? Well, give it time. Find a fine woman, lad, someone with your mother's spirit—yes, I did know her— find that woman, lad, and give the kingdom a twenty-fifth Earl of Kintail. Oh yes, I didn't mention it, Eddie, but I'd like you to be my twenty-fourth earl. It merely involves a bit of paperwork. Are you interested?''

Later, over a second bottle of brandy, the king said, ''You know, Eddie, sometimes it's quite pleasant this being a king.''

WHEN KATHLEEN THRUST THE LIST of instructions into his hands, the old man stiffened visibly. The Earl of Kintail knew that if the terrorists escaped Windsor Castle with their royal hostages, the queen's chances of survival worsened a hundredfold. He faced the young woman impassively and put the list back into her hands.

''I won't do it,'' he said. ''You'll have to get another man.''

''Eddie,'' the queen spoke gently from across the room, ''do as the young woman says.''

''No, ma'am,'' he said. The last word was drowned out by the clatter of the Uzi fired by a terrorist across the room.

Kathleen stepped over the bleeding corpse of the late earl and put the piece of paper into the hands of a horror-dazed young boy.

''Give this to the men outside,'' she said.

The boy who bowed to the queen and left the room, clutching the list of demands in his right hand, was the twenty-fifth Earl of Kintail.

9

Lyons, Blancanales and Corporal Phillips had chased Flynn through a warren of corridors. They saw him as he reached the Waterloo Chamber, but by the time they got there the battle was over. Blancanales had to restrain Lyons and Phillips as shots rang out within the room. Provocation now would only ensure the deaths of the innocents inside.

The three men waited by the entrance. When Phillips's radio intercepted McGowan's voice giving instructions, they pulled back from the entrance, ready to herd the released hostages farther into the private apartments and greater safety.

Two men appeared in the corridor. Instinctively the trio raised their weapons. Just as quickly they lowered them. Blancanales and Lyons recognized Gadgets, and Phillips recognized his CO, Lieutenant Colonel Carlton.

Phillips snapped off a salute to his superior which was crisply returned. The introductions among the five men were brief.

Blancanales placed Carlton's age at somewhere around thirty-five, but it could have been five years either way. The man was in magnificent condition. A quiet fire burned in the blue eyes and beneath the grime of combat there radiated a quiet strength.

Pol's assessment of the lieutenant colonel was cut short by the emergence of the young earl from the chamber. Carlton listened grimly to the boy's message. Then the hostages appeared through the wrecked east door. Carlton called to them and directed the released captives to go to the Green Drawing Room, down the Grand Corridor.

Then he spoke with Able Team.

"The bastards haven't given us a lot of time. I don't know where we'll get a coach on such short notice."

"If that's a bus you're referring to," Gadgets said, "there's one out front. Full of civilians."

"Christ, what the hell are they doing here?" the colonel exploded.

All five of them moved fast down the corridor toward the exit into the Upper Ward. By the time they reached it they were running flat out.

The scene that greeted them in the Upper Ward was organized bedlam. Bodies littered the courtyard—mostly British, but some terrorists as well. The dead were covered in an assortment of blankets. The living were being tended to in the darkness by a corps of civilians.

Near the collapsed Norman Gate, civilians and soldiers worked to move the rubble and free those trapped beneath it. Their efforts were directed by a figure familiar to Able Team, Geoffrey Hall.

Seeing the three Americans, the old man walked briskly over to them and nodded at the bus.

"Best that I could throw together on short notice," he announced. "After our talk this afternoon, I laid in some supplies and borrowed this motorcoach. I thought we might be able to help in the cleanup. From the looks of things, I gather it's not going too well for us."

The stench of burned flesh permeated the night air. The Americans headed for the bus.

Gadgets quickly slithered under the coach to attach something there. He emerged a moment later. "Standard tracking device," he muttered to Hall.

Only moments later Flynn appeared in the Upper Ward. As he passed by the ruins of the King George IV Gate, soldiers and civilians stopped their rescue work to stare at the strutting terrorist. He matched their stares with his own. Uneasily, the British turned back to their tasks.

Flynn reached the bus and checked it out. He put himself behind the wheel and started the engine. He checked the gauges, found a nearly full tank of gasoline.

He radioed the all-clear sign to Kathleen

McGowan and the other terrorists inside the Waterloo Chamber.

The group of hostages made its way to the bus under the watchful eyes of Able Team, Phillips, Carlton and Hall.

"We've lost this one," Phillips murmured.

"The battle only, my friend," Blancanales soothed as the bus pulled away. "Those bastards haven't won this war by a long shot."

10

Leo Turrin had lost all track of time since the snatch. He knew only that he had been taken from the cement room and locked in a small bedroom. No furniture except the bed on which he lay. The window faced a row of other buildings and was barred.

He knew also that he hurt.

Angry red welts on his chest marked where the electrodes had been applied. His muscles ached from the spasms the charges had induced.

Shillelagh's electronic voice had droned on and on, the questions coming at him from all sides. Leo was interrogated by a master. He had been near breaking when two burly men came in through the door behind him, untied him, and dragged him to this room.

He did not know why the questioning had stopped, but he knew that if it started again, he was as good as dead.

He had to escape, and quickly.

The room was no more than twelve feet square, a Spartan cell. Ventilation was provided by a single duct above the door, its grating out of reach, the duct passage far too narrow for escape anyway. The door itself was sturdy, locked on the outside, guarded by a sentry in the corridor beyond.

Leo Turrin was not going anywhere.

The single piece of furniture, a metal cot on which he sat, was hard, unyielding. It reflected his pain, the crazy-quilt of throbs and aches that covered every fiber of his being. Sitting rigid on the cot, acutely conscious of the bare wire mesh beneath him, Leo held himself immobile, shunning any movement that might aggravate his injuries and amplify the pain.

Bastards could have given me a mattress, he groused. Even as the thought took shape he realized there was no time for sleeping or for licking wounds.

Survival was the top priority, and that meant getting out. But how? A rapid visual scan confirmed his first impression of the holding cell: it was a goddamned Mob-style warehouse, plain and simple, with no loopholes even for a man at full capacity. The single, caged bulb overhead illuminated every corner, leaving nothing to the prisoner's imagination, showing him remorselessly that his predicament was hopeless. There was nothing he could use to forge a weapon, an escape tool.

He still wore shoes and socks, slacks, but his torturers had relieved him of his belt and shoestrings—anything that might have served him in the cause of self-defense or suicide.

They wanted him alive and functioning—at least enough to understand and answer questions. Turrin knew they were not through with him by any means. They would be back, and he could not hold them off forever by the force of will alone. Eventually he would break, or he would die. Unless he could devise a method of escape.

Fat chance, the wounded warrior thought. *They haven't even got a keyhole I can crawl through.*

He changed positions gingerly, the effort costing him, and something clanked against his heel beneath the cot. It moved, retreating several inches, scraping over the linoleum with a familiar kind of sound.

Now, what the hell. . . .

He doubled over, peering beneath the cot. It was an empty coffee can, the two-pound size, and Leo had a hunch he had found his makeshift toilet.

On command, his bladder started nagging for attention. Turrin grimaced at the thought of standing up, but Mother Nature had the con and she was calling all the shots. Right now the urge of his bladder was everything, its swift relief his sole objective.

Uncertain that his legs would hold him, Leo compromised by perching on a corner of the cot. With coffee can between his knees, he urinated painfully, relaxing by degrees until the throbbing in his bladder had receded, giving way to other, more persistent pains. About to tuck the can away beneath the bed, he glanced involuntarily inside—and saw the blood that mingled with his urine.

I'm dying here, he thought. *Mack Bolan ain't around to help me this time. . . .*

He had never really thought of Bolan as a savior—though the gutsy blitz artist had saved his ass with frequency enough to qualify by any standard. Going on a lifetime now, Turrin had grown used to thinking of the hellfire warrior, Able Team's mentor, as his best friend, someone to fight and die for if the need arose.

They had not started out as friends, of course. Far from it. They had sworn to kill each other in those days, when Mack Bolan was a soldier freshly home from Nam and taking on another holy war—this time against the Mafia, which Leo Turrin served. It had been close, too frigging close for comfort, right; but after Bolan learned of Turrin's *other* role, his undercover status with a secret federal strike force targeting the Mob, the two men had reached a grim accommodation that had blossomed into spiritual kinship.

And Mack Bolan had been there when Leo needed him, damn right. In Philly, when a double-cross by Don Stefano Angeletti came within a hair of canceling the Turrin ticket—or in Pittsfield, when the war had come full circle with a vengeance! Augie Marinello's boys had stumbled onto Leo's deadly secret, and a life more precious to him than his own—sweet Angelina's—had been hanging in the balance until Bolan tipped the scales. If not for him. . . .

Enough, goddammit.

This time out it was a solo hand for Leo, and he would have to play the cards as they were dealt to him. He could not raise the ante, but he could sure as hell refuse to fold. He had not joined the game to lose, and if it washed out that way in the end, it would not be because he opted for surrender.

Although Leo Turrin did not have the Man in Black to back his play this time, he was not precisely on his own. He had a righteous anger in him, now that he had seen his likely fate spelled out in blood, and there was always that something else—his unshakable belief in justice.

Sure, however outdated that might sound to certain sage philosophers or armchair liberals, for Leo Turrin, justice was the center of it all. He had done time in Vietnam, enlisted with the federal strike force, finally joined Mack Bolan's everlasting war—and all because he believed unswervingly that strong men armed could make a difference. You *could* strike a blow for what was right and fair, for what was just, by God.

And if you got your arms lopped off in the attempt, well then, you started kicking ass until the bastards took your legs away.

Leo Turrin smiled, aware that his condition

and situation hardly made him a champion player.

"Oh, piss," he said wearily.

He glanced down at the can between his feet again, saw red and, in his mind's eye, something else. More softly now, almost with reverence, he spoke the oath again.

Oh, piss.

AT FIRST, the sentry thought he was imagining the sound. A muffled groaning, low, insistent, it demanded his attention like the still-small voice of conscience, long ignored. It came from somewhere close at hand, perhaps inside his skull.

But, no. The groaning was an actual sound, externalized. It issued from behind the door he was assigned to guard.

The sentry cocked his head, one ear almost against the door. No question, it was the prisoner. And he was suffering by the sound of it.

The sentry had observed the captive when they brought him in, and he recognized the signs. The guy was holding up but only just, and from his look, another session like the last would finish him. If the last one had not finished him already.

He was marked for death, this stranger, but the sentry could not let him die just yet. It was his job to keep the enemy confined, secure—to keep him breathing, if it came to that. And he could not afford to let the prisoner check out before his time. If the inquisitors were cheated of their game, they might go shopping for replacements—starting with the man who let the quarry slip away.

His key was in the lock before the sentry hesitated, mulling possibilities. The hostage might be dying. Or he might be waiting just beyond the door, to spring a trap.

With what?

He had no weapons, that was certain, and his injuries must necessarily have sapped his strength. On balance, any small resistance he might offer would be easily overcome.

The sentry frowned, released the strap that held his Colt revolver snug inside his holster. No sense taking chances, even with a man who had one foot inside the grave.

A dying man had nothing left to lose. The sentry, on the other hand, had everything.

FROM HIS POSITION on the floor, curled up into a fetal ball beside the cot, he heard the sentry coming. Leo had his back turned toward the door. He charted the gunner's movements by his footsteps on the bare linoleum.

He heard the door open. His enemy was now over the threshold, maybe ten feet distant.

Still too far.

He waited.

"What's the trouble?"

Leo forced another moan. He was only half

pretending now. The pain was real enough, for damn sure.

Footsteps, and the gunner closed the gap between them by another yard.

Not close enough.

"What is it?"

Leo recognized the edge behind the words. It spoke of tension. A false move now might set the guy off before he got in range, spoil everything.

The hostage groaned again. With feeling.

The sentry was beside him now, the hard toe of a boot against his aching ribs. Leo hunched his shoulder forward, half feigning nausea and sheltering the rancid-smelling coffee can he held tucked in against his chest. A length of heavy wire, which he had freed with difficulty from the cot, was wrapped around his other fist, with seven rigid inches of it thrust between his fingers.

"Speak up, there."

The boot swung in for emphasis and Leo winced, released another realistic moan. When he replied, he kept it breathless, barely audible.

"I need a doctor. . .hemorrhaging inside. . . get help."

He prayed the soldier would not panic and actually go to seek assistance. If the gunner weakened now and showed him too much mercy, he was finished.

Leather—boots and gunbelt—creaked as the

sentry crouched beside him, reaching out to place a hand upon his shoulder.

"Let me have a look."

And Leo let him have it. He was already moving as the hostile hand began to roll him over on his back. His right hand whipped the coffee can around and flung its bloody contents into startled eyes.

The sentry tumbled backward, snarling, one hand clawing at his holstered weapon while the other sought his eyes. Off balance, gagging on the blood and urine that had found its way into his mouth, the gunner landed heavily on his back and missed his draw.

He never got a second chance.

With agile desperation, Leo Turrin lunged, with every tortured muscle in his body crying out, and suddenly he was astride the sentry's heaving chest.

Turrin struck with deadly accuracy at the gunner's throat, his wire lance slashing, penetrating. Razor-tipped and ice pick rigid, it bored through skin and muscle, grating past the larynx, reaming on until his knuckles, slick with blood, were tight against the sentry's jaw. A string of fierce convulsions racked the dying soldier's frame, and Leo rode him like a broncobuster, clinging with his knees, refusing to be thrown.

The sentry took some time to die, his struggles fading gradually, and then renewed for just an instant at the end, as if his dying brain

believed a final savage effort could reverse the
lethal damage, make it right. When he collapsed, the end was sudden, absolute, and Leo
Turrin felt himself alone again inside the holding cell.

He rolled away, unmindful of the pain now,
concentrating on the task at hand. His adver-
sary's weapon had dislodged itself and lay
beside him, inches from his lifeless fingers.
Another moment, and he might have reached
it, might have pressed the muzzle into Leo's
side, and. . . .

Turrin picked up the weapon and weighed it
in his hand. It was a Colt Python, .357 Mag-
num, capable of dropping man or moose at
any range within a hundred yards. He broke
the cylinder and checked the weapon's load,
discovering the sentry had kept the hammer
down on an empty, leaving five rounds primed
and ready.

Leo smiled. The sentry was, had been, a
cautious man. No taking chance with the almost nonexistent possibility of misfires. It was
fortunate that he had been less careful on the
major points, or else.

Beyond his kill, the door stood open, ir-
resistible. The wounded soldier rummaged for
coins in the dead man's pockets, then got to his
feet and stepped across the prostrate body,
moving toward the vacant doorway and the
corridor beyond.

Leo found the stairs. He descended them

slowly, listening for any sound. He was in the main hallway of a small house. The furnishings were simple but spoke of money.

Just as he made the last step, a man came into the hall. Seeing the battered prisoner, the man tried to put down the tray that he was carrying and go for his gun at the same time. To do two things at once proved too much. Flame shot out from Leo's Colt. The bullet slammed into the goon's right shoulder, spinning him into a pirouette.

The tray clattered to the floor with the first shot, and by the second shot, Leo was at the front door. He opened it and glanced behind him quickly for signs of pursuit. He was puzzled that no one came after him, but he wasn't going to stand there and worry about it.

He stumbled into the street.

He didn't care in which direction he went, just so long as it was away from the house.

INSIDE THE ELEGANT TOWN HOUSE, Shillelagh received the last of the report on the assault at Windsor. The interrogation of Sticker had been interrupted earlier this evening when the first reports filtered in from Shillelagh's contact with the CID.

Now two shots told Shillelagh that Sticker was escaping.

Obviously, the man he had set to guard Sticker had been careless. His carelessness had been doubtless terminal. Shillelagh could do nothing.

In addition to Shillelagh and Sticker, there were only two men in the house, both part of Shillelagh's hard arm. Any force larger at this particular house would have drawn the attention of the authorities.

Leo's escape was an inconvenience. Shillelagh picked up the telephone. Long manicured fingers dialed, then a device held tightly to Shillelagh's throat sent eerie directions into the night.

As HE WALKED ALONG the street, the cold crept up on Leo as his exhilaration at escaping wore off. He had no protection against the cold, he was still without a shirt. The Colt was tucked into the waistband of his pants. People walked by him, stepping out of the way of the wild man with the red welts.

He found a phone booth outside a subway station. Leo peered at the instruction card, took out a handful of the coins liberated from the guard, and dialed 100.

The operator came on, and dialed the American embassy for him. He had no idea how much she told him to deposit, he just fed all the coins into the box.

"Get me Sir Jack Richardson. This is Sticker."

"Good God, sir," the embassy operator exclaimed. "Sir Jack isn't here at the moment. He and half the embassy are out looking for you. Where are you?"

"A subway station. The sign reads Ravenscourt Park."

"Right. Sir Jack's not too far, maybe five minutes away. Stay there and I'll call him."

Leo hung up the phone and collapsed. His knees gave way and he sank to the floor of the booth. He was totally beat.

From across the street, two men in a station wagon watched him slump. They got out of the vehicle and fanned out, alert for any friends of the prey.

A moment later, one of the men had disarmed Leo and was dragging him struggling to the parked car. His companion watched for interference.

Constable Brown had patrolled the Ravenscourt Park area for most of his working life. It was a quiet district; in fifteen years he had seen very little that had made him truly scared.

He had just turned into King Street when he saw the two men. Constable Brown called out to the man to release his struggling captive.

The lookout hesitated too long. By the time he had swung his weapon, Brown was rapping his club across the guy's wrist. The gun skittered across the pavement. A billy-club blow into the lookout's stomach had the guy doubled over.

Mustering his final reserves of strength with fierce determination, Leo reached back and delivered a roundhouse right to the nose of the man who held his left arm in a vicelike grasp. The man reeled as much in surprise as from the force of the blow. Leo took the advantage and grabbed his Colt back. He fired two shots into the guy's chest. The corpse collapsed in a gory heap. A pool of blood quickly spread.

Constable Brown looked at the disheveled fellow he had just helped rescue. The man looked like hell.

"Well, you had to shoot him, I suppose," the constable sighed. He held the captive lookout by the scruff of the neck.

A limo cornered heavily at the end of the street. It roared up, then slammed on its brakes to stop parallel to Leo and the bobby and his prisoner.

Armed Marines from the embassy force spilled out of the car and surrounded the three men.

It took Sir Jack Richardson a moment longer to get out of the car. The cane kept getting in the way. He raised himself to his full height and marched toward his American colleague and the two strangers, one of them regrettably a policeman.

"Let me see your permits, please!" boomed Constable Brown, his eyes bulging at the man with the cane and at each and every one of the Marines. With his prisoner still securely accounted for by the neck, he prodded the Marine with the nightstick as Leo laughed. "You first, soldier. Your papers where I can see 'em, and put that thing *down*!" he snapped, rapping the man's rifle barrel with his stick.

Sir Jack Richardson watched. It was going to be a long night.

11

Three Bell UH-1D helicopters settled down onto the south lawn of Windsor Castle. Rocket packs were mounted on the sides of each. As the rotors slowed, a U.S. Army officer clambered from one of the Hueys and approached the nearest group of men.

"Major Sam Johnson reporting. I'm looking for Able Team."

Pol Blancanales identified himself as Able Team.

"My orders are simple," the major said. "Do what I'm told, when I'm told to do it. Sorry we took so long getting here."

"That's all right, Major," Blancanales said. "There wasn't a damn thing any of us could do. But we can use you now."

Major Johnson smiled, pointed to the idling helicopters. "An M-60 on each side, sixteen 2.75-inch rockets in the packs. Armed like in Nam...."

THE THREE HUEYS FLEW WEST, just beside and above the A40 highway to Oxford. Major Johnson flew nearly at treetop level in the night, following the blip.

"Any chance this could turn into a fire mission?" he asked Blancanales.

"Yeah," Lyons replied. "It's very likely."

Johnson's copilot interrupted. "Major, the signal indicates the bus has stopped."

Johnson brought the Huey to a hover, radioed the two other gunships, asked Blancanales for instructions.

"What sort of country are we in, Major?"

"Farm country, sir. There is some urban buildup, we're just west of High Wycombe."

"Then you must guide us to where the bus is. You must put us down within a half-mile of it."

Johnson sent the Huey farther down the A40. Within two miles he veered to the right, reported that he had reached position. Johnson maneuvered his gunship over a field of barley and set the chopper down amid swaying grain.

Three men stepped into the field, and headed toward the bus.

KATHLEEN MCGOWAN WAS HOME. Home being, in this case, a hardsite. Scattered around the perimeter were members of the Irish Freedom Army. Roving patrols checked on the sentries at irregular intervals, the irregularity of the visits keeping the sentries alert.

The thirty hostages had disembarked from the bus right after Kathleen. She pointed them toward the farmhouse under the watchful eye of men toting weapons with 75-round drums, a demonstration of massed firepower.

Then McGowan spoke briefly with several patrol leaders. The leaders headed away to roust more troops to protect the farm.

She entered the parlor of the two-story stone house to find that her fellow terrorists had split the hostages into two groups. One of the groups, consisting of twelve hostages, sat in the middle of the floor of the empty living room. Five terrorists with Uzis and AK-47s kept their guns trained on the group. The remaining hostages, including the queen and the princes, were put in what had been the dining room under heavy guard.

Kathleen nodded approval, and headed up the stairs followed by Joseph Flynn. Both had borne the brunt of the night's work, and now they wanted only to sleep.

Looking from an upstairs window, Kathleen watched as two of the terrorists put the bus inside the barn. The fit was tight, but they got inside and closed the doors. That job completed, the two men returned to their patrol.

THE NIGHT WAS STILL as the men worked their way toward the farm. Their black suits were invisible in the night. Two British soldiers who followed at a distance blended in nearly as well, their lighter uniforms melding into the golden shafts of grain around them.

Guided by triangulations radioed from the

two helicopters, the five men crept into a large field that abutted a farmhouse.

Using his Startron, Blancanales picked out perimeter guards. Lieutenant Colonel Carlton also appraised the defending forces.

"Those roving patrols are a problem," Carlton whispered.

"Our biggest problem is locating the hostages," Blancanales responded.

"Quiet probe," Lyons said.

"Let's do it," Blancanales agreed.

They signaled the two British soldiers to back off. Able Team lay prone, modified Colts held at full extension; accuracy was essential. They aimed into the darkness of the field.

The three autopistols, set for single shots, sneezed three .45-caliber bullets.

Two terrorists on roving patrol spun quickly, minus lower jaws, their mouths and throats ripped away. A third fell straight back with a hole above his eyes.

Before the two surviving patrolmen could react, the next trio of slugs hit. One crushed a larynx, another an eye that it drove into the brain. The third slug hit the same man in the bridge of his nose.

The corpses fell silently to the soft earth.

The three Americans had created their opening. Five raiders went through it. The attack team advanced into the blackness.

12

In twenty seconds, the gunships would be moving in to take care of the troops in the yard. To avoid being chewed up in the impending slaughter, the raiders had to be inside the farmhouse when the gunships hit.

Fifteen, fourteen, thirteen....

Phillips tapped Blancanales on the shoulder and pointed to their left. Blancanales saw two approaching terrorists. The terrorists still had not seen the raiders.

Ten, nine, eight....

The terrorists never would see the raiders. Three .45's from Pol's Colt sailed into them like angels of death.

Five, four, three....

Blancanales did not wait to see the two corpses fall. Already they could hear the rotors of the three gunships roaring into M-60 range.

Two, one....

Blancanales and the British corporal ran toward the side of the house as the choppers opened up on the troops gathered in the yard. Blancanales reached for a stun grenade, pulled the pin and lobbed it through a window, shattering the glass. The grenade was quickly followed by one from Phillips. As the first grenade burst, Lyons and Gadgets dashed for the front of the house.

The Hueys' M-60s raked through the terrorists.

Terrorists fired back from the barn where the bus had been parked.

Major Johnson brought his Huey in and delivered eight rockets to the barn. The structure exploded in a ball of fire, the rockets igniting the fuel in the bus. Three terrorists emerged from the inferno, burning like torches.

Christ, thought Kathleen McGowan, staring at the headless remains of Joseph Flynn as she hid behind the smoking remains of the barn.

She ran the length of the barn toward the open field. Someone saw her, friend or foe, and suddenly a mass of pellets tore through her insides. The shooting triggered more shooting as the remaining terrorists opened fire in panic on anything that moved. The raiders, too, joined in the mayhem, but with purposeful precision.

Outside the battle was over.

PANDEMONIUM HAD ERUPTED in the two rooms where Blancanales's and Corporal Phillips's stun grenades had burst. A stun grenade explodes without shrapnel. The flash temporarily blinds anyone within a confined area. The concussion can cause deafness. In every way, stun grenades disorient the enemy.

Gadgets on one side of the door and Lyons on the other poked their Ingrams through windows and sprayed the walls at chest height. Nine millimeter slugs stitched through plaster and flesh alike.

Under the cover of the fire, Blancanales and Phillips slammed the door open with their feet and rolled into the room. Phillips's Sterling barked twice, delivering death both times. Four fell in the dining room under Blancanales's onslaught.

Lyons squeezed the trigger of his M-16 and carved a figure eight into everything before him. He caught a hint of movement at the top of the stairs to his left, and rolled as a 7.62mm slug plowed into the hardwood floor where he had stood a heartbeat earlier. More slugs slashed the floor as the burst from the top of the stairs continued. Then the gunner fell, and the staccato challenge ceased as abruptly as it had begun.

Lyons looked into the dining room. The hostages cowered behind a young man holding a smoking Uzi. The Uzi pointed directly at Lyons.

Carlton's voice called from the open window. "Your Highness, he's one of us."

The young prince looked unblinkingly at the intruder.

Lyons nodded to a nearby youth holding an AK-47. "Friend of yours?" Lyons asked the prince.

"My brother."

"Take my M-16," he said, tossing the weapon to the younger prince. "It looks better on you." He admired the two young aristocrats for their alacrity in securing guns from the dead and protecting the other hostages.

The other hostages included the Queen of England. The regal lady, her tawny suit marked with dust, stepped forward from within the group to confront the stranger in the blacksuit, who used his Ingram to cover the scene before him.

"Why your black uniform? Who are you?"

Donald Fagan's penetration of her palace in 1983 might have shaken the queen, but nothing had prepared her for the horror and carnage that had scarred the most recent hours of her reign. Abducted from a palace filled with bodies chopped by gunfire, terrorists and soldiers alike draped bleeding over the furniture, then herded into a farmhouse that came under attack from missile-firing helicopters, she stood at last under the suspicious gaze of a blacksuited man waving a gun. It took all the stamina she possessed to come forward with her head high.

"I demand to know who you are," she said to the stranger.

"Lady, I haven't got the time," Lyons said.

A good-looking man stepped forward. "Mother—"

The queen signaled him not to interrupt. She was still in control. She repeated her question to Lyons, adding, "Whose side are you on?"

"If I was a bad guy, you'd be dead by now."

The prince bridled at hearing his mother addressed with such lack of respect. "Are you some sort of American mercenary?" he said.

"Mercenary?" Lyons sneered contemptuously. "If a man fights only for money—" he swept the snout of his weapon to indicate the smouldering corpses outside "—he won't go the last mile for you. Maybe you wouldn't understand."

The prince stared back into the cold steel of Lyons's eyes.

The queen headed off a clash between the two men by shaking her head in resignation. "Is there to be no end to this killing?" she intoned softly. "Does peace demand such a bitter price?"

Lyons looked at her. "You can only hope for peace," he said levelly, "if you can bring yourself to understand war."

"You are an intentional and emotional berserker!" huffed the young prince. "We do it different over here."

"I kill people who don't give other people respect," Lyons shot back. "We're not so different."

"All you talking of is killing. . ." the prince replied.

"If you want peace," Lyons explained, "you must understand war. You must understand the organization of violence. You must know why men fight. It's a bloody game and mankind has had a long time to practice it. We are much better at waging war than making peace.''

The prince revealed a respect for the American's words. ''Madam,'' he said to his mother, using the formal term in order to seek permission, ''I must go with these gentlemen. I believe they can use my contacts and influence to track down the perpetrators.'' The young man's eyes were eager.

Lieutenant Colonel Carlton addressed the queen from the doorway of the overcrowded room. ''Your son tells the truth, Your Majesty. We must act fast. We need access and influence, starting now. I will ensure His Royal Highness's safety.''

The queen glared at Lyons. ''If word of *any* of this should ever leak out....'' She hesitated; she did not even know the stranger's name. Lyons looked back over his shoulder as he left with the lieutenant colonel and the prince.

''I'm sure not going to tell anybody, lady. Are you?''

13

The three men of Able Team, Corporal Phillips and His Highness went directly to the U.S. Embassy. There, Able Team and Phillips changed into civilian clothes. While they changed, Sir Jack Richardson briefed the five men on Leo's kidnapping and Ripper's death.

Leo met them all in a study downstairs. He appeared shaken. But his physical wounds were minor compared to the wounds on the inner man. He had very nearly broken under the unremitting questions of Shillelagh's electronic voice; the knowledge that only fictional heroes are able to completely resist torture did not make him feel any better.

Scotland Yard had raided the interrogation house in Chiswick—and found nothing. The dead tagmen had disappeared, and the floor of the room where Leo had been kept was spotless. All traces of Shillelagh and the operation had been removed.

Leo listened in as various options for nailing Shillelagh were discussed by the hunters. Finally Gadgets spoke. His words were clear but cryptic.

"I say we bug 'em all."

"Corporal Phillips," Blancanales said, "are there any good electronics stores around here?"

"Several. But none are open this early."

"No problem," Lyons volunteered. "We just do a little midnight shopping."

"Your Highness, you may not want to hear this," Gadgets told the prince.

"Oh, I doubt I would want to miss such a fine example of American ingenuity," the young man said.

Gadgets grinned. He started making out the shopping list.

Within minutes the men had selected a car from the embassy pool of vehicles.

The shoppers found what they were looking for on the Edgeware Road: an electronics store that dimly displayed a supply of basic components.

Corporal Phillips pulled the station wagon over to the curb and remained behind the wheel. Lyons and Schwarz got out and checked the street. Only an occasional car passed.

Seeing no pedestrians or cops, the two men signaled Phillips and the car pulled away. Phillips would circle the block at regular intervals until he saw one of the men back on the street.

Gadgets went boldly up to the front door and located the ancient alarm. He disarmed it by attaching a piece of wire to the alarm connection visible between the door and the jamb. When he broke the connection, the alarm tickled only the ground, not any rusty bells. Lyons expertly picked the lock, and the two men slipped into the store.

Aisle after aisle of equipment was spread out in front of them. Gadgets worked his way up and down the aisles, occasionally picking up an item. His pencil flash fell across silicon chips, microphones, circuit boards. Some of them found their way into his bag.

Lyons saw movement on the street and hissed a warning to his shopping partner. The pencil flash blinked off. Gadgets dropped behind one of the rows of cases. Lyons crouched directly below the window ledge. The light from the cop's flashlight came perilously close to Lyons's huddled form, but he was out of the policeman's line of sight and the light moved on. The door rattled slightly as the cop checked it was locked.

Lyons and Schwarz waited two minutes before peering out from their hiding places. Then Gadgets double-checked his list and made a rough estimate of the price. He pulled out a wad of bills, counted some out, added twenty percent as a fudge factor, and left them with the list by the till. The two men waited for Phillips's return.

When they spotted the car's headlights, Lyons calmly left the store. Schwarz emerged with his bag. He rearmed the alarm system and joined Lyons in the car. Phillips smoothly pulled away from the curb and headed back to the embassy.

Blancanales, Sir Jack Richardson and the prince had been busy. They had worked out a plan whereby all seven of them would split into three teams. Sir Jack and Carl Lyons would keep Leo's appointment with Lady Carole Essex. Phillips and Gadgets would don telephone-repairman uniforms and bug the residences of the members of COATUK. Blancanales and the prince were to visit the empty offices of certain key individuals and leave a few of Gadgets's "souvenirs" at each stop. Leo Turrin would remain at the embassy, to coordinate the three teams' efforts.

Gadgets set up shop in another part of the embassy and assembled a dozen miniature microphone-transmitters and an equal number of receiver-recorders. He also started a small collection of telephone taps. Three hours later, he pushed himself away from the table and examined his handiwork.

The microphone-transmitters were small enough to fit comfortably in the pocket of a suitcoat, and their self-adhesive backing would stick to anything solid. The microphone was ganged to the short-range transmitter, which contained voice activated circuits. When the signal was received from the microphone, the transmitter boosted the signal and sent it to the receiver-recorder.

The receiver-recorders, only slightly larger than the microphone-transmitters, could be operated anywhere within a one-hundred-foot radius of the transmitters.

Wherever he found himself in the world, Gadgets Schwarz would always end up better equipped than when he arrived....

14

Lyons and Sir Jack left to keep Leo's appointment with Lady Carole Essex. They were rigged for the street. Lyons suspended the M-10 on a Desantis shoulder rig underneath his suitcoat that made the weapon instantly accessible. Attached to the strap of the Desantis was a modified military holster that held the Colt.

Sir Jack had a similar setup for his Uzi. His hand weapon was Ripper's Beretta.

The meeting was set for a bookstore on Cecil Court, a short street that ran between Charing Cross Road and St. Martin's Lane in the very heart of London. Lined on both sides with antique shops, Cecil Court was a magnet for collectors of all kinds.

The limousine pulled up to the old bookstore. Lyons stepped onto the pavement and checked up and down the street. He signaled Sir Jack who clambered clumsily out of the car. The door slammed, and the vehicle continued on down the street. The Marine driver had instructions to circle until the two men came out.

A bell over the door tinkled as the men stepped into the store's musty interior. Lyons looked around him. The store had evidently not changed much in about a century. Books lined all of the walls from floor to rafters, with more on shelves built over a doorway that led into the back of the shop.

The proprietor came out from the back as Sir Jack browsed among the books. Half-moon glasses perched on the end of his nose, he stooped slightly from spending a lifetime bent over the volumes that passed through his shop.

"May I be of some service, gentlemen?"

"No, thanks, just browsing," replied Sir Jack.

"Certainly. If I may be of service, please call."

With that the man stepped back to give them the run of the small shop. Their eyes turned as the bell rang and a petite blonde entered the shop.

Clearly Lady Carole was known here. The proprietor reappeared and was about to greet her when she held up a hand to silence him. Turning to Sir Jack, she showed concern in her expression at the presence of Lyons.

"He's with me," Sir Jack said.

"James, would you please leave us alone for a few moments?" Lady Carole requested.

The old man bowed slightly and retreated into the shop's back room.

"From what Mr. Sticker told me, Sir Jack, I hadn't expected you for a while."

Sir Jack Richardson filled Lady Carole in on Leo's kidnapping.

"I'm afraid that I haven't been able to find out much more about Shillelagh," was all that the lady volunteered. Her coolness worried Sir Jack, who asked her some more questions, then set the date and time of a later meeting.

When she left the store, Lyons came up to Sir Jack. "Did you notice she didn't ask if Leo had told Shillelagh about her? Surely she'd be worried about having her cover blown...."

In a flash, Lyons was at the door, scanning the street for Lady Carole. She was just turning the corner into Charing Cross Road when Lyons spotted her.

He turned to Richardson. "Sir Jack, get to the car. Call Leo on the carphone. I'll stay in touch with him on my radio." Then he took off after Lady Carole.

The car came to a dead stop in front of Richardson. He climbed in the back. He picked up the phone and called Leo.

His narrative was interrupted several times as Leo got directions over the radio from Lyons. Then came the last direction. "Lost her in Leicester Square. Damn. Have Sir Jack pick me up. Out."

BLANCANALES AND THE PRINCE had just returned to the limo from their second stop when Lyons's call came through. As they sat in their car, their own mission temporarily on hold, Blancanales discussed the situation with the young royal.

Then His Highness slid back the divider between the front and back seats and gave the chauffeur instructions for their next target.

A few minutes later, the big car pulled up to the Victoria Street entrance of New Scotland Yard. The two men got out of the Phantom VI and headed inside.

The individual they had come to see was Chief Inspector Bruce Stewart, head of the CID's counterterrorist division and that agency's representative on COATUK.

Stewart had a reputation for being highstrung but a good leader. Since the formation of the counterterrorist force he had risen from heading up a small group of Special Weapons Officers to become head of the entire department. He was definitely a target for a bug.

His Highness and Blancanales walked into the reception area of Stewart's office. The secretary turned from her typing to greet them and stared in disbelief at the young man whose face she knew from a generation of newspapers.

"I'd like to see Chief Inspector Stewart—now please," the young man commanded.

"Certainly, Your Highness. I'll announce you."

In a moment, Stewart came out. Blancanales sized the man up. Stewart shook hands with the prince and ushered the young man toward his office.

Since the prince had made no move to introduce his companion, Stewart assumed that Blancanales was a bodyguard. Pol sat down in the reception area. The secretary asked him if he would care for some tea. He answered with a grunt. Taking the hint, she returned to her typing.

Blancanales reached into his pocket and took out a receiver-recorder. Surreptitiously he removed its backing and stuck it to the underside of the chair.

The secretary was glancing nervously at the door to Stewart's office. The sound of His Highness's voice occasionally penetrated to the outer office. Clearly, the young man was upset about something.

The sounds of talk died as a visibly upset Stewart emerged from his office and asked his secretary to bring in tea.

It was while Stewart was away from his desk that His Highness stuck a microphone-transmitter to the underside of it. When Stewart returned, he saw the young man hunched over tying his shoelace. Then the young prince rose.

"I don't want tea—I want answers," he stormed. "Clearly, I am not going to get them here. Good day, sir," the prince snapped as he stormed out of the office, collecting Blancanales in his wake.

Back in the confines of the car, the American congratulated the prince.

"Hell of a performance, Your Highness," Blancanales said with a smile. "Damn good show."

GADGETS AND CORPORAL PHILLIPS, disguised as telephone repairmen, set about placing a microphone-transmitter on the home telephone of the Secretary of State for Northern Ireland. To give their cover credibility, Gadgets took the simple expedient of knocking out phone service to several of the houses in the neighborhood.

Phillips then went to the door of each of the affected houses. Dressed in dark blue overalls, he checked out the house's telephone. Earlier in the morning, Gadgets had shown him how to take one apart, tinker with it and put it back together.

The cover established, Phillips called on the Secretary of State's home. A butler led the corporal to all of the phones in the house. But instead of leaving, the butler hovered by Phillips, making it impossible for him to plant either of the two bugs he was carrying. He cursed as he came out of the house to report his failure to Gadgets.

"We'll plant an outside tap," Gadgets said. He scaled a telephone pole, using the appropriate equipment.

It took Gadgets five minutes to install the tap. When he was done, he climbed back down the pole and returned with Phillips to the truck.

As Phillips drove, Gadgets consulted the map of further targets.

It took them just under two hours to plant all the bugs, both internal and external.

Then they had to retrace their route and proceed at a crawl past each target, so that the receiver-recorders could collect. They did so in less than ten seconds per transmission.

On returning to the embassy, Gadgets copied the collected tapes and divided them up among the seven men to listen for information. The process was a tedious one. After an hour, all the voices sounded the same.

But Leo found something that made him rewind the tape. The voice of Chief Inspector Stewart came through the cassette-player's small speaker.

"I don't care what it takes. I want a meeting today...."

"Okay, the Preston Road place," said the voice on the other telephone. "And I'll make sure that Shillelagh's there."

The battle was on. Able Team left the room with Corporal Phillips.

A tired Turrin stayed behind with Richardson and the prince.

"Sir Jack, I think it's about time we taught His Highness to play poker," Turrin said.

"How about it, Your Highness?" Sir Jack asked.

"Only if I can deal first," the young man replied. He took the deck from Turrin. "I'd like to play a game I learned in Mexico," he said, shuffling the cards expertly. "It's called five-card Texas hold-'em. Do you know it, Yank?"

15

Preston Road was in the heart of Kenton, a small suburb northwest of London.

Shops lined both sides of the street for about four blocks. Beyond the shopping area, Preston Road was lined with single family homes.

The four warriors, dressed in civvies, SMGs suspended in Desantis rigs, autopistols secured in modified holsters, extra magazines for the weapons weighing down their suitcoat pockets, drove slowly along Preston Road. They spotted a police cruiser parked in front of one of the small, Tudor-style houses.

Phillips drove the Ford Granada past the house a little way and then parked. Getting out, the four headed back toward the house. When they reached it, the front door opened.

Recognition flared in Stewart's eyes as he spotted Blancanales, the Prince's bodyguard from that morning. The four men scattered as Stewart ducked back into the house.

Lyons ran toward the narrow passage on one side of the house, Blancanales toward the other, both men unholstering their Colts. Gadgets and Phillips barely made the shelter of the police car as the first shots came from the second-story window.

The side windows of the Ford dissolved under the fusillade of 7.62mm and 9mm missiles. Gadgets and Phillips covered themselves as pieces of safety glass rained on them.

Gadgets crawled toward the front of the car. Phillips pulled out a Beretta and worked his way toward the rear of the car. He popped his head over the trunk long enough to dispatch three 9mm discouragers toward the house. One man was terminally discouraged with a 115-grain slug through the junction of his neck and shoulder, severing his jugular.

Gadgets's silenced Colt sighed once and the .45 met a face at another window. The face disappeared in a pink mist.

More gunners trained onto the car from the first-floor windows. Phillips pulled back, but not fast enough. He grunted as a 7.62mm slug found his right shoulder. Gadgets moved to him as Phillips tore at his shirt to make a bandage. Schwarz finished the job and hurriedly tied the bandage into place.

Rounds from the house continued to puncture the side of the car. It would not be long before they found the gas tank.

"Can you move, Phillips?"

"Yeah—but where to, mate?"

Gadgets holstered the Colt and pulled out the Ingram. He helped Phillips holster the Beretta and remove the Uzi from the Desantis.

"We're retreating, to the front."

Gadgets poked his head up and sent a burst from the Ingram toward the front windows of the house. Phillips pulled himself up and started to run toward the front door. A burst from his Uzi kept their opponents' heads down. Three heartbeats later, he collapsed against the house, with Gadgets a heartbeat behind him.

An AK poked out over the window ledge, seeking the two men. Gadgets fired his M-10 straight up, slugs finding the man's hands. The assault rifle dropped as its former owner screamed in his retreat.

Gadgets looked at Phillips's expression of pain. "We'll rest here for a couple of minutes."

Phillips nodded, leaned back and adjusted his blood-soaked bandage.

LYONS ROUNDED THE CORNER of the house just in time to see the fat old cop called Stewart running toward the gate to the back lane. Three silent .45s splintered the wood of the gate, and Stewart rolled to the ground. When he turned from his roll, his fist held a Browning that spat flame at Lyons.

From the other side of the house, Blancanales saw the cop fire. He wanted Stewart alive. He took his Colt in a two-handed grip and squeezed off a .45. The slug tore into the meaty part of Stewart's left leg. He lost the Browning in his surprise.

Lyons ran to the downed cop. A spray of slugs from the house sought him and he had to dive for the cover of an oak tree. Stewart was not so fortunate. Bullets found several vital organs, ensuring his permanent silence.

Lyons pulled out the M-10 and sprayed .45s across the second story in three-round bursts. He quickly changed magazines and kept firing as he saw Pol working his way along the house toward the back door. A head briefly peered over one of the windowsills on the lower floor, only to disappear again as Lyons directed a blast of fire at it. Lyons ducked behind a tree, 7.62 missiles from the second story smacking into trees all around him.

Blancanales made the back door. Lyons jammed in a third magazine, fired two more bursts and left the cover of the tree to join his partner.

Blancanales fired into the latch and his partner hurled himself at the door, diving into the kitchen. To his right, a shotgun blasted. Lyons sent three rounds into the gunner, finding the man's belly.

A few of the shotgun pellets had burrowed into Lyons's side, but the full blast of pellets had found one of the other terrorists. Blood sprayed the kitchen walls.

GADGETS CHECKED PHILLIPS. The corporal was losing blood quickly. But the assault could not wait.

Gadgets aimed his M-10 at the door. Beside him, Phillips joined the blitz. The two men stormed the door simultaneously, firing at the lock and doorknob.

The door swayed inward. Gadgets pulled back quickly as bullets whistled past him. Staying low, he swung in front of the door, loosing a hail of .45s from his M-10.

The opponent within caught two bullets, one in his shoulder, the other in his right knee.

Gadgets and the corporal charged into the house. Only the groaning of the wounded man greeted them.

Catching movement, Gadgets spun and was about to pull the trigger. He saw Lyons and Blancanales emerging from the kitchen and lowered his weapon.

Lyons looked at the man on the floor. Kneecapping was a favorite method of terrorist torture. This was poetic justice.

"Let justice take its course," he muttered to himself as he stepped over the man and headed cautiously upstairs.

Blancanales and Schwarz joined him in the post-battle reconnoiter. Lyons poked his head above the landing. Finding the hallway empty, he continued to the top of the stairs.

Carefully the three men moved from room to room. Corpses lay in poses of death in different rooms.

The three men descended the stairs, Lyons trailing his two companions. The screams of the kneecapped terrorist had turned to low moans.

Lyons leaned down to speak to the injured man.

"I have some questions that you're going to answer."

He did not need to say any more, he simply moved his hand toward what was left of the man's knee.

"Ask, for Christ's sake, ask me anything," gasped the terrorist.

"Where's Shillelagh?"

"Went to the basement when the shooting started. Stairs are in the kitchen."

Lyons leaned on the right leg slightly as he straightened up. He looked at Corporal Phillips, who sat in a corner of the room, eyes closed.

"Just the three of us, then," he said. Blancanales and Gadgets joined him as he moved into the kitchen. They saw a partly open door.

Blancanales and Gadgets took up positions on either side of the door. Lyons swung it open. When no fire came up the stairs, he gingerly headed down, one step at a time.

He reached the bottom of the stairs. The basement was empty. He called to Gadgets and Blancanales. They leaned into the doorway and went down the stairs.

"Nothing here," Lyons said. "Let's get some help for Phillips, then check in with Leo back at the embassy. And I'll deal with our kneecapped friend upstairs myself...."

16

Lyons brought the Granada to a stop in front of the hotel on Sussex Gardens. The hotel was an old house that had been converted into a hotel just after the Second World War. It was what the English called a "bed and breakfast"—cheap but clean accommodation. It was here that the American specialists would connect with vital information. Leo's contact, Lieutenant Colonel Carlton, had come up with the likely whereabouts of a certain lady, thanks to more loose talk caught by the bugs.

The three men of Able Team climbed the hotel's steps and rang the front door bell. A woman in her late sixties opened the door.

"May I help you, gentlemen?"

Blancanales spoke. "We're looking for Lieutenant Colonel Carlton."

"Ah, you must be George's American friends. Do come in."

She led them to a small living room on the first floor in what was obviously the owner's apartment. Carlton was seated in one of the overstuffed armchairs. He rose when the woman came in with the three visitors.

"My mother, gentlemen," he said as she left. To Blancanales's unspoken question, Carlton continued, "I bought this place for her a couple of years ago. It provides a small income, and she enjoys mixing with all the tourists. As it was convenient, I thought that we could meet here, keeping you off the streets and out of trouble—if that's possible."

The three men hovered uncomfortably in the room. They were in their blacksuits.

"We shouldn't have to wait," continued Carlton. "Several of my men are taking turns watching the place from a café across the street. Her hideout is located in a long stretch of Westbourne Terrace. The building is four stories and contains several apartments. The top two floors are luxury flats, and we have established that Lady Carole secretly owns one of these."

The colonel's radio, on a table next to his chair, crackled to life.

"Colonel, a lady matching the target just entered the building," a voice said. "You may want to come and check this out."

"Right, gentlemen," Carlton said, standing up. "Shall we be off?"

Westbourne Terrace was one of the principal streets in Paddington. The stone building where Lady Carole maintained her lair was obviously well-cared for, the exterior free of the black soot that scarred so many of London's older buildings. The door was well-secured against any casual intruder. But these were no casual intruders. Carlton brought out two keys.

"Got these from the landlord earlier today," he whispered. He opened the door and they entered.

They avoided the elevator and worked their way up the stairs. With a click and a whir, the elevator started up and the warriors retreated into the shadows as the old cage-type elevator descended past them. The four men checked out the occupant. The woman did not resemble Lady Carole, and as the elevator sank down below the second floor, the four men returned to the stairs and climbed to the third floor.

Lyons cautiously poked his head around the corner of the corridor, quickly pulled it back. There were two men on either side of a door-way.

The two guards were alert, and one of them had seen Lyons's head. Footsteps sounded as the man came to investigate.

Lyons brought up his silenced Colt. He saw the barrel of a gun precede the guard around the corner. The four men waited in silence for the rest of the man, a brief wait before he cautiously peeked around the corner. The Colt sighed, and the bullet all but tore the cautious head off.

Before the body had even hit the floor, the four invaders were around the corner and a slug from Gadgets's Colt had slammed into the second guard.

The door to a nearby apartment opened and a head looked out. Blancanales tracked onto the head, refraining from pulling the trigger.

A gray-haired man gazed horror-struck at the four men and retreated into the shelter of his apartment. Blancanales stuck a foot in the door, preventing it from closing completely. While the man appeared to be an innocent, Pol had to check him out. Quietly, the senior member of Able Team forced his way into the apartment.

"What are you doing?" the occupant demanded, terror in his voice.

"Just checking things out—nothing to worry about." Blancanales barged past the man and charged from room to room. In one of the upstairs bedrooms, he found the man's wife getting ready for bed. She screamed at the intruder, and Blancanales beat a hasty retreat—closely followed by a flying hairbrush. He returned downstairs.

"Sorry for the intrusion," he said to the old man. "You and your wife must stay inside, and away from the front door of your apartment."

To confirm the wisdom of the American's advice, sounds of pitched battle penetrated from down the hall.

Carl Lyons had gained entrance to Lady Carole's place by firing three .45s into the door latch. A shotgun had boomed at him from within, sending pellets crashing into the swinging door. Lyons dived low into the apartment, M-10 spraying as he went.

A second shotgun blast shredded the couch he hid behind. Its stuffing exploded into the air.

Lyons crawled to the end of the couch. He heard the sound of the shotgun being broken open.

Gadgets came in low, sending a spray from the Ingram toward the sound of the shotgun.

The gunner did not hear the smack of the bullets as they slammed into him. He heard nothing but the roar of the emptiness of death.

Gadgets rolled to the couch and took in the apartment as he did so.

The white, well-decorated room stretched thirty feet to the left. Stairs led to the apartment's second floor at the far end.

Silence filled the place, ominously. Blancanales peered cautiously around the door, gun-muzzle preceding his eye. He saw the splattered blood spots on the white carpet.

Lyons and Gadgets cautiously worked their way toward the stairs.

Blancanales joined Lieutenant Colonel Carlton and they moved to back up Schwarz and Lyons.

The two men in the lead stepped silently along the corridor at the top of the stairs. There were four doors in the hallway, two on the right, one on the left and the last at the end of the corridor. Lyons and Gadgets placed themselves on either side of the first door on the right.

Lyons slowly turned the handle. When no shots greeted him, he pushed open the door. It was a bathroom. Lyons entered and pushed aside the shower curtain. Nothing. The room was empty.

Blancanales and Carlton checked the door on the left. Pol pushed it open slightly. It slammed shut on him, bullets drilling through the white-painted wood. Splinters sprayed as Blancanales leaped back. Carlton groaned as if hit. Then he opened up with his Sterling, stitching a figure eight in the closed door.

Blancanales kicked open the door and dived in. His caution was unnecessary. On the floor beside him lay a moaning figure doubled up on the floor. The guy fought a losing battle to stuff entrails back inside a 9mm zipper across his stomach. The man stared at Blancanales, then his eyes glazed over and he fell silent.

The last door on the right was already partially open. Gadgets opened it the rest of the way. Silence met him, and he walked in unopposed. The room may have been a bedroom once, but it was a study now. Two filing cabinets stood along one wall, with a desk and chair in front of them. The place was meant for work and nothing else. It would have to be checked out thoroughly—later.

Lyons stared at the remaining door. Suddenly he snapped a new magazine into place and pulled the trigger. A three-round burst at the lock blew the door open.

Carlton moved to one side. Blancanales to the other. Gadgets rolled into the room. He was nearly cut apart by a stream of submachine-gun bullets.

The bullets tracked across the floor, trying to find the rolling figure.

Lyons stepped through the door and gave the M-10 its head.

Silence descended on the room as the dust settled. They were in the upstairs master suite. Gadgets sheltered behind a divan. Lyons had thrown himself behind a tub chair.

Off to the left was the open door to the dressing room where the submachine-gun fire had come from. Signaling Blancanales and Carlton, Lyons covered the door as the two men stepped into the master suite and moved toward the dressing room.

Blancanales looked into the small room and saw flapping curtains. He checked it out. A fire escape.

He cursed.

17

Noisy chaos greeted the four men as they left the building. Police were everywhere, trying to control the curiosity seekers who had gathered at the sound of gunfire. Some of Carlton's men were helping the bobbies keep the crowd away.

Able Team stepped back as three of Carlton's men moved past them with a curt nod. The Americans recognized some of them as they headed up to secure the apartment from intruders.

Lyons paced away from the crowd with Carlton. "Where the hell do we look?" he said.

"We look in the alley that leads to Paddington Station, that's where," Carlton grinned. A glint of triumph showed in his eyes. The nearby railway station was the ideal bait for their prey.

Lyons waved to his partners. The three men jogged after the English soldier who knew the mean streets and alleyways of London like a coroner knows the arteries of a corpse.

They turned sharp right at the end of the

street into an alley connecting with the wider pedestrian alleyway that ran behind the row of houses. In the main alleyway, about a hundred yards to the left of them, the pursuers saw the small, unmistakable figure of Lady Carole Essex. Unmistakable because she walked briskly, as if to avoid attention.

The pounding of boots on the pavement alerted her. She looked over her shoulder and broke into a run at the sight of the four men.

Lyons broke ahead of the sprinting group. He chased the woman as she darted into a side alley that dead-ended fifteen feet from her turn. He had her cornered.

He crouched, looked at his quarry to catch sight of any firearm in the darkness.

She showed no weapon. She had sunk to her knees on the grimy cobbles, leaning her head against the brick wall that blocked her way. She was whimpering.

Lyons rose and turned to address Schwarz and Blancanales. "She's mine," he said softly to his partners. "Leave her to me."

He entered the dead-end alleyway and stepped remorselessly toward the petite blond woman. She let out a scream.

He took a last long, quick step up to her. "Shut your cake hole, dammit," he told her. The muzzle of his Colt touched her forehead.

She choked off her scream, stared up at him like a terrified dog, the tears in her eyes catching the starlight. But this was no mongrel. This bitch was class.

"Why did you do it?" interrogated Lyons. "Why did you get them to take so many hostages?"

"I had nothing to do with it!" she yelled back at him. Her pretty face twisted into ugliness with fear and rage. She clutched her handbag to her chest like a crucifix. "It was the Irish that did it. Irish terrorists. I'm not Irish—"

Lyons shoved his weapon into her right cheekbone and pushed her face sideways against the bricks. Nerve endings in his flexed right forearm told him the venomous kiss of the Colt was only seconds away.

"Why?" he repeated. "Tell me why." His tone condemned her as surely as the hangman's grasp on the trapdoor lever. "Tell me. Now."

The woman's cowardly collapse before him enraged Lyons.

"Listen to me, woman. This gun in my hand—I call it my roadblocker, see? Nobody goes anywhere when I've got this thing pulled. So talk. It's all you've got left," and he pushed the barrel up under her top row of teeth, forcing her mouth into a grotesque leer.

She backed away from the muzzle as far as she could, which was less than half an inch. With the gun pointing at her palate, she gasped a defiant confession.

"If I'd killed them all, I'd have had the succession. I'd have been queen for a day, pretty boy. Maybe queen for a lifetime!''

"You're crazy," Lyons pressed. "Twenty dead people and the next in line would have been suspect number one."

"But I was going to be hit, too, jerk." She laughed crazily, saliva splashing from her immobilized mouth. "McGowan would have staged an attack on me as well."

"Then that's the way it's gonna be," Lyons said without emotion. "You're going to be hit too...."

"No!" she screamed, cringing. "Don't do it! I beg of you!"

"Lady," Lyons said once again, "I don't have the time."

As his finger pressed on the trigger, Lady Carole shoved the barrel from her mouth with the handbag. Desperately, insanely, she rummaged in the bag for her handgun. Lyons eased up on the finger pressure. He let her find what she sought.

The woman pulled a small caliber piece from the bag and pointed it at her assailant.

Just as she pulled the trigger, Lyons's Colt boomed. The point-blank explosion thrust the woman's small gun under her disintegrating chin, where it discharged in turn.

Lyons's blast had taken her face away, but her own shot creased what remained of her forehead and took off her hair.

Lyons looked aghast as the dead woman's

wig flew from the pulpy head to reveal a hairless skull covered in scabs and sores.

The faceless nonbeing lay crumpled in a heap at the bottom of the wall. The woman had been fearfully sick before she died. Cancerous lesions of the skull stood exposed to Lyons as he backed away from the remains.

His partners joined him. The mouth of the small alley filled with curious soldiers and police.

"Good diagnosis, good treatment, Doctor Lyons," Gadgets joked without smiling.

"And in the best tradition of British socialism," observed Blancanales, "she got it free."

18

IT WAS NOT OVER for Carl Lyons. The shooting of the Shillelagh woman had disturbed his whole being.

Asleep at the U.S. Embassy four hours after the hit, he thrashed about wildly on the bed. Suddenly he awoke in a sweat. The action on foreign soil—maybe killing the woman—had set it off again.

He was scared. And he knew damn well what caused him such fear. A recurring nightmare haunted his sleep since his woman—*his* woman—had met her death. The dreams filled him with horror, especially since the nightmare was different each time. Each hideous experience was a variation on the death of Flor Trujillo. . . .

This time he knew the gunman would follow Flor to the airport, that there would be yet another death. In the dream, he leaned against a row of lockers and scanned the crowd.

He saw Flor as she approached the metal detector at the entrance to the waiting area. She was beautiful. Not sick, not crazy, not violent. Just a totally beautiful woman. She joined the group of travelers already in the line. She was last. Lyons watched. From time to time she craned her neck to look through a huge plate-glass window at the planes on the tarmac.

Lyons could see the runway area through the window. The brightly painted Ecuatoriana Airlines jet looked like a Chinese paper bird in his dream. He saw the fuel attendant remove the nozzle of the hose from the plane's fueling port.

Then it was Flor's turn to go through the detector. Once Flor left the departure area, she would be safe.

The gunshot thundered in the confines of the glassed-in corridor. The slug lifted Flor onto her toes.

Even in death she was spectacular. Her exquisitely sculpted calves stood out fiercely as she rose on tiptoe. Thigh muscles strained against white cotton walking shorts. Well-shaped buttocks clenched.

Lyons watched her back arch slightly, her arms upraised as purse, passport, documents flew out of her hands.

Then she crumpled to the floor. He rushed from cover, panning his revolver across the hallway.

Nothing moved. People lay flat the entire length of the corridor. Slowly he let his arm fall as he stepped backward to where Flor lay.

She was lying on her side on the grooved rubber mat of the departure-lounge entrance.

Lyons knelt beside the inert form. He turned the body onto its back. He looked at her fine Hispanic features. He saw her full lips, cherry red with blood, touched with a hint of a smile.

Something slammed into his gut so hard that Lyons thought he was hit. Then he recognized the pain for what it was.

Lyons, awake now, moaned to think of Flor. The woman was the only person with whom he had shared his soul. Lyons hurt inside for his mother also, dead for ten years. She had known nothing of the good life, nor had she expected it. Lyons cried inside for his drunken father who achieved with his loins what he had failed to achieve in a wayward and vagrant life, and thus presented Carl to the world.

Finally, Lyons wept for himself, the lonely adolescent, the sad teenager who closely guarded his every step upward, afraid it would be taken away from him. He did everything right, followed all the rules. That was why he had become a policeman.

Lyons remembered target practice at the LAPD training academy, the first day in the shooting booth when he thought he'd blown his chance to become a cop and make something of himself.

As the dummy popped up before him, he started shooting at the head. For a fleeting instant he saw his father's face on the cardboard cutout. Lyons kept squeezing the trigger until there were no bullets left in the pistol. He continued to squeeze the trigger, again and again, until the weapons instructor tapped him on the shoulder and told him to quit it.

From that day, he understood the degree to which he must contain the rage within him.

As a member of Able Team he had demonstrated on occasion a volcanic nature that made his two colleagues shake their heads. Now he struggled to relax and empty his mind in a land far from home where once again he had acted like a raging storm.

One battle was over. But the battle within him would never be done.

EPILOGUE

The military jet warmed up outside the hangar as the Americans shook hands with a small group of people.

Leo Turrin, his head wrapped in bandages again to conceal his identity during the drive from London, looked forward to the bandages' removal on the plane, though they would have to go back on before he disembarked.

"Right to the last you fed lies to Shillelagh, Mr. Sticker!" Lieutenant Colonel Carlton shouted above the whine of the aircraft's turbines. "You held out. You're a tough bugger! I have a souvenir for you, my friend."

Leo accepted the odd device from the colonel. It looked like one-half of a telephone receiver. "What the hell is this?"

"Turn on the switch, hold the large part to your throat, and whisper."

"Like this? Oh, shit!" he exclaimed, in the distorted electronic voice that had tormented him in that room.

"It's used by people who have lost the use of their own voice," the colonel said. "That's how she managed to protect her identity for so long—she dealt with most of her contacts over the telephone.''

Minutes later, the Americans gave a final wave to their British colleagues and boarded the waiting aircraft.

THE AIR FORCE JET hammered through clouds. The green checkerboard grid of the British countryside had ended abruptly as a meandering white ribbon of foam marked the start of the English Channel.

The plane streaked on a course due southeast.

Only two men on the aircraft knew their destination: the pilot and Leo Turrin.

Turrin had just finished his report on the Windsor Castle hit to Stony Man Farm. Now he pondered the information given in exchange.

The destination data he had passed on to the pilot. Behind him he heard the lighthearted banter of the men of Able Team.

He understood the relief the warriors felt at wrapping up this foreign mission successfully. He wondered if the men could stand the strain of their next ordeal. Turrin did not envy the trio as he thought of the hostile terrain of the Hindu Kush.

Who in hell was The Dragon?

White House liaison Hal Brognola, usually an eloquent man, had begun hedging and stuttering as he gave Turrin the mission data from the Farm. He had sounded preoccupied. Turrin was especially puzzled when the head Fed said Stony Man was having a bit of trouble.

Leo was certain it was nothing that the gang at Stony Man Farm could not handle.

At their first refueling stop in Rome, Turrin would inform the men of Hal's phone call. Then he'd switch to a commercial jet for Washington.

The three Stony specialists would continue to New Delhi. There they'd meet with the contact man for a briefing on this next hit. Brognola's words rang in Turrin's ears: "Leo, I'm sorry to put Able Team on the spot, but we're after a man called The Dragon who runs a show from a fortress in the Hindu Kush. If Carl and the guys can stop him, then we'll cut off the arms supply to nearly every terrorist group there is. That's all I can say for now, except that I trust your discretion about when you choose to tell them."

"Hey, Leo, get your head out of the clouds and c'mon over here!" Turrin twisted in his seat to see Gadgets Schwarz waving him over.

The men were crowded around a tired Carl Lyons. The tall blond man, fatigue showing on his face, held a rectangular box.

"Okay, let's see what she gave us," Schwarz said.

"She? Who?" asked Leo.

"She sent us this," Lyons said, lifting the box.

"For cryin' out loud, Carl, who?" grated Leo. "What's in it? Open it up."

Lyons spoke as he removed the box top and revealed tissue paper within. "The queen got them from the estate of the old Earl of Kintail—you remember that kid? Well, his father was a pilot during the Battle of Britain. It was a custom. The aces collected these from their dead comrades and treasured them. A way of honoring their courage, I guess."

"So what's in the damn box?" Leo seethed.

Lyons opened the tissue paper. He held up four silk scarves.

"For a queen," Lyons said, looking around at his friends, "that woman is a real prince."

A bonus for Able Team readers:
Early Fire
Deep background on Able Team's mentor,
featuring Mack Bolan in Vietnam

Mack Bolan was tired.

It had been one hell of a night.

He and Sniper Team Able had penetrated deep into Vietcong-held territory. The mission had been a success. Two VC chieftains and two string pullers from up north had gone down. The kills had been quick, four head shots as the targets stood around a fire. Then Bolan and the team had begun their withdrawal.

There was a skirmish with another band of VC coming in from patrol. But Sniper Team Able came through all right.

Long months in Vietnam had honed their survival instincts. They had even begun to think like the Vietcong.

Now five men trudged wearily into the Special Forces base camp at Cam Lo.

Zitka and Bloodbrother, the scouts; Gadgets Schwarz and Rosario Blancanales, the flank men, and Bolan.

Sergeant Mack Bolan.

The leader of Sniper Team Able.

Zitka and Bloodbrother gave Bolan the thumbs-up sign and joined Gadgets and Pol on their way to some much-needed sack time.

Bolan was covered in sweat even though it was a relatively clear, cool night. This was rice country and the paddies were almost dry. They were like mud flats. The combination of the boot-sucking terrain and the dikes sapped their strength, making each forward movement laborious. All this, compounded by the tension inherent in a mission behind enemy lines, had made for an exhausting trek.

The CO's orderly spotted Bolan from across the compound and hurried over, his face anxious.

"Sarge, Lieutenant Colonel Crawford wants to see you. Right away."

Bolan nodded. "I was headed that way, Corporal."

So the old man was waiting for him. That was no surprise. The colonel always waited up, like a father worried about a son who stayed out late.

The young "penetration specialist" smiled at the thought. The colonel could never take the place of Sam Bolan, back in the States. But Crawford had been observing Bolan's progress and had taken Bolan as a green recruit and taught him what he needed to know to survive in this damn war. Not only to survive, but to give his best.

Bolan walked by a private with an M-16 pulling guard duty at the door of the HQ Quonset, and went inside.

A thin-faced E-3 sat at a desk in the outer office pushing papers.

Bolan nodded to him and raised an eyebrow, jerking a thumb at the closed door of the colonel's office.

The sergeant shook his head and started to say something.

Before he could get a word out, the door burst open.

The prettiest whirlwind Bolan had ever seen exploded out of the colonel's office and ran smack into him.

The woman looked about twenty-three with a shock of chestnut hair and a face that was startlingly attractive. She wore fatigues and from her shoulder hung a camera and a compact tape recorder. Piercingly blue eyes stared in anger at Bolan, then dropped to the black lettering on an O.D. green name tag on his tiger-striped camou fatigues.

"Sergeant Mack Bolan?"

"That's right."

"The one they've started to call the Executioner?"

Scorn dripped from her words.

Bolan shrugged, suddenly wary.

"I've been called that."

Colonel Crawford appeared in the doorway of his office at that moment. He ignored the woman and returned Bolan's salute.

"Come in, Sergeant. Welcome back. Come in and report."

With hands on hips that shapeless fatigues could not disguise, the woman persisted in questioning Bolan.

"A successful mission, Sergeant?"

A live wire, thought Bolan.

Feline fury flashed in her eyes.

"That's classified, lady. Excuse me."

"How many babies did you kill? How many women and old men?"

The words slashed at him like an invisible bayonet, but he kept his face emotionless and his mouth shut.

"I, uh, see you've met Miss Desmond," Colonel Crawford said dryly.

"We haven't been formally introduced," grunted Bolan.

The woman stuck her hand out. "I'm not afraid of a little blood, Sergeant. Jill Desmond. I'm a—"

"Journalist," Bolan finished for her.

His fingers closed over her hand. The gesture was brief, cool.

"Miss Desmond's here for a close-up of the war," the colonel said. "I've told her what they told her in Saigon. Our operations in this area are highly sensitive."

"I'll bet they are," snapped Jill Desmond. "That's why I'm here. I've had enough brass to get this far, Colonel. What makes you think I'll stop now? This is where the real dirty work goes on, out here in the boonies. And I'm not going back until I've seen it for myself, so I can tell the people back home what it's really like. They deserve to know.''

"I'm not denying that, Miss Desmond—'' the Colonel began.

"You're not trying to cover up the crimes of men like Sergeant Bolan here, are you?'' She glanced at Bolan. "There's a reason they call you the Executioner, isn't there, Sergeant?''

Bolan studied the woman's face. She seemed intelligent, but you sure couldn't tell it by the accusations, the lack of understanding, the naiveté.

"I'm going to find out the truth about this war.'' Jill Desmond bristled. "Not the white-washed official version you people are peddling.'' She swung around to face the colonel again. "Then I'm going to tell everyone who'll listen just what a barbaric, immoral thing this war really is.''

She flicked one more morally outraged glance at Bolan, then stalked out of the Quonset.

"If we were barbaric murderers,'' Crawford grunted as he and Bolan stepped into his inner office, "I wonder what makes her think she'd be safe?''

"She doesn't know the jungle yet,'' agreed Bolan. "But she *cares*. She's all right.''

"Yeah, but she makes it harder for us to do our job,'' the colonel reminded him. "Speaking of which, have a seat and report.''

Bone weary, Bolan settled into a chair across

the desk from the colonel, who nodded as Bolan related the kills in the village and the firefight in the jungle afterward.

"Good work, son," he said when Bolan finished. The corners of the CO's mouth drew back in a grimace. "You must be damn tired."

"I could use some sleep," said Bolan, shrugging.

"Wish I didn't have to tell you this after a mission like that, but there's no ducking a bad job, I always say."

Bolan waited, trying to ignore a foreboding in his gut.

"Sir?"

"I can't send Jill Desmond back to Saigon, much as I'd like to," Crawford growled. "I've got orders from the top to cooperate with her."

"She must have a lot of pull back home."

"Enough. Anyway, she's here for as long as she wants to stay. And while she's here, I've got to have somebody I can trust keep an eye on her."

Bolan's mouth tightened.

A baby-sitter.

The colonel wanted him to baby-sit the live-wire journalist who had a mad-on for anything military.

"I, uh, could think of better choices for the job than me, sir."

The CO chuckled.

"I'll bet you can, but I can't. The lady

doesn't seem to like you, Sergeant, and I don't blame you for not liking her, but if anybody can keep her alive while she's out here, it's you.''

"Is that an order, sir?''

"It's an order.''

Bolan stood.

"Then I guess I'd better catch up with her and get her locked up somewhere for the night.''

"Just don't let her know that she's locked up.'' Lieutenant Colonel Crawford chuckled. "She was mad enough when I told her I was going to assign someone to keep an eye on her while she's here.''

Bolan's mouth quirked.

It might have been a smile. He saluted and started to turn when Crawford stopped him.

"Sergeant, you might tell her what the Viet civilians call you. Sergeant Mercy fits you just as well as the Executioner.''

"She wouldn't understand,'' Bolan said simply.

He reached for the doorknob. It was jerked open before he could grasp it.

"Well, what is it, Corporal?'' the colonel barked at the orderly who barreled into the room. "You'd better have a damned good reason for not knocking!''

"It's Miss Desmond, sir,'' the corporal said, shakily. "The reporter.''

"I know who she is. What about her?"

Bolan had that foreboding in his gut again.

"She's taken a jeep, sir. No one expected her to try something like that. It was parked behind the motor pool. They worked on it today. Uh, gave it a tune-up and everything. C Company was supposed to pick it up first thing in the morning."

Crawford slammed his fist on the desk top.

"Damn. What do you mean she stole a jeep?"

The corporal cowered. "She was gone before anybody knew it. She headed west."

"West? Toward Three Click Fork?"

The corporal nodded again.

Bolan sighed as he thought of Three Click Fork, three kilometers from the camp where an old supply road branched north and south.

Where the heaviest concentration of VC activity in the area was reported to be building up.

That was the intel from all the recon patrols.

A bad place for an unarmed, just-off-the-plane reporter who also happened to be a woman.

A terrible place.

"Sergeant?"

Bolan glanced at the colonel and nodded.

"On my way, sir."

Bolan stalked out into the jungle night.

So Jill Desmond wanted to know what war was really all about.

The Executioner hoped she wouldn't find out.

The hard way.

SOLDIERS.

They were all alike, Jill Desmond thought as she piloted the bucking jeep along the road leading away from Cam Lo base camp.

They were like juvenile college boys in a fraternity with their secret handshakes and rituals.

They didn't want to let anybody in on what really happened, least of all an uppity woman who had "no right" to be there.

Well, Lieutenant Colonel Crawford and his bloodthirsty Sergeant Bolan were wrong if they thought they could keep the truth from her.

She was young, yes, but she was also damn good at her job.

She was more than willing to wade through any kind of shit to get the story she was after.

The camp was one kilometer behind her.

The twin beams of the jeep's headlights cut through the curtain of night, revealing the deeply rutted road.

She jerked the wheel savagely and geared down as the vehicle bounced over the crater-pocked roadway. With each depression in the half-paved track the jeep threatened to head into the jungle.

This wasn't any worse than the road she had

driven over in the hills of Kentucky when she interviewed the leader of that cult. He had been a little scary with those burning eyes, that long beard, the shotgun in gnarled hands.

Then there had been the Black Panther she had ventured into Watts to find. She had gone to places where a white woman had no business. She had asked the questions nobody asked, and she had survived.

She had flourished.

Guts.

That was all it took. If you had guts, you could go anywhere, do anything.

There were no sounds of war in the jungle night as she drove through its velvet blackness.

She would find the people who lived in this area. She would ask questions. The truth would be told.

The people back home were starting to wake up to what the truth about Vietnam really was. The human suffering. Napalm. The fat cats.

War was always good for business. Young men were dying in a rich man's war 10,000 miles away from home. Most of them had no idea why they were there, fighting a people who had done nothing to them. They weren't heroes, they were pawns in the wrong place at the wrong time. The first real rumbles of protest were beginning to be heard.

The truth would fuel those protests, and that knowledge made her job simple.

Find the truth.

Get it to the people.

Cam Lo was two clicks behind her.

Men like Mack Bolan had free rein to kill and maim and torture, and their superior officers hung medals on their chests for it.

Somebody had to put a stop to it before this backward little country was overrun with self-styled Executioners.

The glow of the headlights washed over Three Click Fork.

Jill Desmond stopped the jeep.

A frown marred the smoothness of her forehead.

She had pored over maps of the area before coming out here and had expected this fork, but she wasn't sure which way she should turn.

There were villages in both directions.

She tromped on the gas and spun the wheel to the right. The vehicle headed north down the narrow road.

As she drove, she tried to recall the smattering of Vietnamese she knew. Many of the villagers, especially the elders, knew English, she'd been told. She was sure she would be able to communicate with them.

The truth has a way of breaking down most barriers, including languages.

The harsh growl of the jeep's engine sounded loud in the night, drowning out the many little jungle noises that whizzed by along both sides of the open vehicle.

But the jeep sounds did not drown out the

sudden burst of rattling gunfire from up ahead.

Instinctively, Jill hit the brakes.

The jeep skidded to a stop.

She sat very still, not realizing she was holding her breath.

The weapons fire continued.

She could distinguish the crackle of small-arms punctuating the heavier blasts.

She cut the jeep's headlights but left the engine running.

Her eyes adjusted to the darkness. She saw a flickering brightness up ahead, around what was evidently a bend in the road. The glow was red, licking the night sky as she watched.

Fire.

The village was being put to the torch!

She was too late!

Already American and Army of the Republic of Vietnam forces were moving into the village, razing it. Probably because the villagers had the audacity to resent the way their country, their lives, were being invaded by corrupt foreign governments. Maybe the civilians had provided food and shelter for the Vietcong.

This was it.

Her response was automatic.

She reached down on the seat beside her for the tape recorder and camera.

This atrocity would not go unrecorded, unpunished.

This one would see the light of day.

She unfastened the flap of a pack and took out her equipment. Then she took a deep breath and got ready to start down the road again. She would proceed on foot, even though that would be tricky.

Continuing in the jeep would present an easy target. She would be more likely to get shot.

The jungle pressed in close on both sides of the road.

Jill Desmond was about to step down from the jeep when a hand reached out, grabbing her arm.

She screamed into the night.

Jerking around, she saw a face looming at her out of the darkness: flat features, lank black hair, cloth tied around the forehead.

Vietcong.

Reflex took over.

Jill's foot left the brake, slammed the gas pedal. She popped the clutch.

The jeep shot forward.

She was thrown back against the seat.

The VC let go.

The left front wheel of the jeep dipped off the roadway. The lurch threw Jill heavily to the side.

She grabbed for the wheel, straightening herself and the jeep. Her foot was still on the gas. She left it there. Keeping her head down, she drove, her heart pounding wildly.

Somehow the jeep stayed on the road.

She heard firing from behind her.

From the sound of it, there were at least two or three others back there with the man who grabbed her, triggering shots after the fleeing vehicle.

A slug ricocheted off the body of the jeep with a whining spang.

Jill cringed, feeling the first tinge of fear.

She barely made out the bend in the road in time to whip the jeep around it, rather than crash into the culvert dead ahead. Once she negotiated the turn she brought the jeep to a halt.

Her jaw dropped at the scene of carnage spread out before her.

Unimaginable carnage, everywhere she looked.

The hooches of the village were grouped in a rough circle. Beyond them was the thick blackness of jungle night.

This had been a peaceful place once.

But no more.

All the huts were ablaze. Villagers ran around in frenzied shocked, scared confusion. Smoke and gunfire filled the air.

Jill saw an old man stumble out of one of the flaming huts. He was on fire.

Watching in numb horror, Jill saw a young woman race through the night with her baby clutched to her chest. The fire cast a red glow over her terrified face. The mother's face disappeared in a spray of blood. She had run into a bullet. The baby dropped shrieking from her arms, into a puddle of mud.

The villagers were being driven from their homes like stampeding cattle by the torches of soldiers. The civilians were being systematically slaughtered.

Then she saw the black pajamalike "uniforms." Not ARVN. Not soldiers, as Jill had thought.

Vietcong.

She saw at least two dozen VC firing into the village. Sometimes they shot to kill, sometimes only to disable. Then they would finish the job with the long knives they carried. The firelight glinted on the hacking, bloody blades.

A VC toting a machine gun raked fire across a fleeing knot of civilians, stitching them, shredding flesh, pulping bone. Bodies erupted gore.

Jill Desmond was sick.

Deep-down sick. Far past the vomiting stage.

A tiny moan escaped her throat.

It was stilled by the cold touch of metal that suddenly pressed against her temple.

"Do not move," a heavily accented voice growled close to her ear.

Jill did what the voice told her. She remained still except for the trembling that she could not control, spasming up from her gut.

The man holding the pistol moved around to her side. In the reflected glow of the village's destruction, she could see him.

The face was lean, skin pulled taut over high

cheekbones. Dark eyes glittered with the light of madness. No. Not madness.

Savagery.

He wore a crude uniform and was evidently the leader of this group of VC who had surrounded the jeep. His eyes took in every detail of the newswoman.

A razorlike smile slit his face.

"American," he said softly, the comment almost lost in the clamor of gunfire and screams from the village. "Very good."

The Cong leader stepped back and motioned curtly with a pistol. Two of his men stepped toward the jeep.

Jill shrank from them. Her mouth moved.

"No," she whispered. "Oh, God, no...."

They grabbed her arms, yanking her from the jeep.

She screamed in pain. Her cries were ignored.

Thirty seconds later, the jeep stood deserted in the road.

The VC vanished into the jungle with their captive.

Bolan ignored his weariness.

This was his first tour of duty in Vietnam, his first experience with war, but he had already learned to push himself beyond the natural limits of endurance. His life depended on it.

He was still in camou fatigues, but he had

traded his sniper rifle for an M-16 equipped with noise-and-flash suppressor. A .45 automatic nestled in leather on his hip. Grenades were clipped onto the belt around his waist. A long double-edged knife was sheathed behind the .45.

He moved on foot along the road, traveling at a good clip. He was a moving shadow, nothing more. He knew that he could cover ground almost as fast as the jeep. He reckoned the disrepair would slow Jill Desmond's progress.

This way was quieter.

He heard the gunfire to the north. He stopped. He listened.

It could be a firefight between VC and American forces, but the young combat specialist doubted that. The VC had "liberated" lots of French and American weapons over the years.

Bolan launched into a jog again.

A few minutes later he reached Three Click Fork.

The firing to the north had died down.

Bolan hesitated only a fraction of a heartbeat, then headed in that direction.

Everything was quiet to the south. He eliminated that possibility.

Bolan had to follow his instincts.

They told him that Jill Desmond had turned north. That she was right in the middle of that trouble up ahead.

God help her.

Before he had gone very far, he spotted the glow of the fire through gaps in the trees, growing brighter as he advanced.

Running directly into hell.

He saw the deserted jeep.

Bolan went into the brush at the side of the road in a rolling dive, came up with the muzzle of the M-16 lined up on the vehicle. His finger rested on the trigger, ready to send death down that road at the first sign of danger.

After a long moment he let out his breath again.

There was no movement around the jeep.

Bolan came out of his crouch and hurried on to the vehicle.

He drew up beside the jeep...and stared past it at images out of a lunatic's nightmare.

Destruction was everywhere.

What had been a peaceful village hours ago, when Able Team had passed through on their way home, was a blood-drenched hellground. Corpses everywhere. Corpses of every age, both sexes.

Sporadic firing broke out. A few VC darted around the flaming ruins of the huts, finishing off the survivors of the massacre.

A mop-up party.

A larger force had done this and had left.

Jill Desmond wanted to learn the truth about the war.

There was no better place.

The Executioner got to work.

One of the villagers, a man whose legs had been shattered by bullets, lay on the ground, pleading for mercy from the black-clad VC who loomed over him. The VC's grinning face became a devilish mask in the glow of the firelight as he lifted his knife, ready to chop.

His head exploded in a shower of blood and gray matter. He pitched backward in a death sprawl.

Bolan tracked right, squeezing off another round.

Another of the bastards went spinning into oblivion as a slug punched open his head.

Two more VC went down before the others realized someone in the shadows was sniping at them. The ones still alive cast about frantically for some sign of the wraith-like, silent sniper.

Shouting in anger, one of the VC peppered the nearby jungle with rounds from his machine gun. He was kicked backward an instant later by a burst that splattered through his neck.

Another threw a grenade into the trees.

Bolan was on the move and out of range by the time it exploded. The Executioner dropped the grenade thrower with another short burst from the M-16. He slammed another clip into the assault rifle and wiped the sweat from his forehead with his sleeve.

He stayed on the perimeter of the village, always on the move, pausing every few feet to deliver death to another of these vermin who preyed on their own countrymen.

He had to take one of them alive, so he could find out where the others had taken Jill Desmond.

He snapped off another shot. A running Cong flopped to the ground. Bolan scanned the area.

There had to be at least one more VC around here. There had to be.

Bolan moved out from the tree line.

In the darkness he heard the snap of a twig to his left.

He slipped to the side as automatic-weapon fire ripped through the space where he had just been.

The muzzle-flash came from near one of the burning huts.

Bolan put a round through the ambusher's chest and another through his thigh. The VC fell, weapon spinning away. He sprawled on the ground thrashing and sreaming in pain.

He was still alive.

Bolan stepped forward.

The wounded VC fumbled for a grenade.

Bolan's booted foot lashed out and broke the man's wrist. The grenade bounced away harmlessly, pin intact.

Bolan pressed the muzzle of the M-16 against the guy's chest.

"I hope to hell you speak English."

The Cong's eyes were wide, filled with terror. But he did not respond.

Bolan switched to Vietnamese. His fair command of the language got his point across.

The guy twisted his head back and forth in response to Bolan's question. The fear grew stronger. So did the pain as shock wore off. Blood leaked from the corners of his mouth. His breathing was harsh, ragged.

Bolan asked once more where the others in the group had gone.

Again the man shook his head.

Bolan's eyes darted around the burned-out village, looking for any sign of Jill Desmond.

Nothing.

She was gone.

Taken.

A coldness grew inside Bolan, a white-hot coldness.

He thought about what would happen to the woman if she remained a VC captive for even a short time.

Then he shifted the M-16 and pressed the hot muzzle against the sweating forehead of the wounded creep.

For the last time, Bolan asked his question.

This time, the guy answered.

"Xan Lung!" he screamed out.

Bolan eased off the pressure of the M-16 threatening to blow the guy's skull to bits. He stood, trying to decide what to do with the man, when the VC made the decision for him.

The VC scrambled as fast as he could toward a fallen machine gun, dragging his shattered leg behind him. He got his hands on the weapon.

Then Bolan's burst from the M-16 ripped the VC apart.

The Executioner was alone in a village of death.

He drew a long breath and let it out slowly. Fatigue tried to claim his body and soul. But he refused to acknowledge it.

Time to get moving.

The nights were never totally quiet.

There were insects and other small creatures moving through the jungle. The sounds of nature went on.

The path Bolan followed was narrow and winding, the bushes around him so thick that only the smallest glimmer of moonlight penetrated.

He moved by instinct most of the time, hurrying along the trail at a soundless jog, the jungle fighter in his element.

He quickly circled the perimeter of the decimated village before leaving it behind, and his first thought was confirmed.

Jill was not among the dead.

The VC had her.

They could make use of a captured American, especially an attractive female journalist.

There would be more than the inevitable

rape. They would debase her totally as a woman, as a human being.

Mack Bolan was not going to let the woman die.

He stepped up his pace.

With his rifle at the ready, his combat senses fine tuned to danger in the jungle around him, he hustled along.

The wounded VC back at the village had told him with two words where the others had gone.

Xan Lung.

A village one hour to the north that had already felt the purging touch of the VC. They had taken over the village, constructed a munitions dump there. They abandoned the settlement when the Americans learned of the VC presence and shelled the area.

The village was well off the main "highway."

Bolan headed in that direction, making his own path at first, then following the trail he came across. He was fairly sure that the VC had used the path earlier that night. An occasional vine that had been hacked away from the jungle trail told Bolan that the wounded man had not lied. The VC *had* come this way.

With Jill.

The path was muddy in places. The muck suctioned at his boots. The ever-present stench of decayed vegetation filled his nostrils, making the air thick.

The sound of voices came to his ears.

Bolan slowed.

The voices were low pitched. The source was ahead of him, just off the trail.

He melted into the bush on the same side of the path and stood absolutely still. His alert senses had saved him from walking directly into a security perimeter. He heard two voices, conversing in Vietnamese.

Okay.

If they were lookouts, they weren't very good ones. Deep in the jungle, though, he supposed it was easy for them to get overconfident.

He moved up on them so softly that not even the night creatures were disturbed.

Within moments he was a few feet from the enemy but neither of them had any idea of his presence.

One of the VC laughed at a comment from the other one.

Bolan knew he had to take out both of them almost at the same time to prevent any outcry.

He rushed forward between the two of them. Surprise registered on one of the men's faces, but not for long as Bolan rammed the M-16's butt sideways. There was a cracking sound as skull bone shattered. One VC, dead on his feet, stumbled back, blood spurting from his nose and mouth.

The other man only had time to emit a startled grunt. He started tracking his rifle upward, but the Executioner pivoted in a lightning-fast maneuver and swung the gun stock again. The second VC, his head caved in, dropped lifelessly to the ground alongside his comrade.

Bolan left them there.

A few steps and he was back on the trail.

Where there was one set of guards, there would be another.

Bolan advanced a few meters, then left the trail. The going would be slower, but he was willing to sacrifice a little speed.

Long minutes passed as the nightscorcher made his way through dense clinging undergrowth.

A whiff of cooking came to him, intermingled with the usual smells of this jungle world.

The VC camp at Xan Lung.

Suddenly a guttural voice challenged him.

Bolan dived forward, somersaulting and coming up in a crouch. He spotted the shadowy bulk of a sentry in the darkness and triggered off a round.

The silenced assault rifle chugged.

The figure in the shadows staggered, clutching at its middle, and fell.

Bolan moved to the man's side, knife unsheathed, poised.

The VC was dead, drilled through the heart.

Bolan drew a deep breath.

He moved forward on his belly, leaving the dead sentry behind him.

Another few minutes brought him to his goal.

Bolan huddled in the thick choking growth and peered out into a clearing that was illuminated by a small fire.

There were at least fifteen Vietcong in the camp.

Some of them were drinking, some were gathered around a cooking pot suspended over the fire.

Most of the huts that made up the village of Xan Lung had been destroyed, but a few were still scattered around the clearing.

Dominating the scene was a bombed-out concrete building—the abandoned munitions dump. Parts of it had been leveled by American shelling. Sections of the roof had collapsed, but the walls still stood for the most part.

Bolan's eyes flicked from figure to figure down there, checking out everyone.

There was no sign of Jill Desmond.

She was either inside one of the huts or inside the munitions dump.

Or she was dead.

A choked scream from the munitions building gave Bolan his answer.

There were too many of the enemy for a grandstand play to be successful.

Unless it was one hell of a grandstand play.

He circled the camp, encountering no more lookouts. They had to feel secure; this was their territory.

Bolan returned to his original position at the back of the munitions dump.

There were three sentries posted behind the building. They looked none too alert, though, and they were huddled fairly close together. That would help.

The sentries laughed and talked among themselves as they passed around a liquor bottle.

Bolan hoped the noise of their voices would be enough to cover up what happened next.

Bolan raised the M-16.

He squeezed the trigger.

He did not see the bullet zip through the eye of one guard. He was already tracking to the next, firing again.

The second man kicked into a loose death sprawl. He hit the ground a split second after the first.

The third sentry actually got his mouth open to yell as he tried to bring his weapon up into firing position.

Bolan sent a slug sizzling into that open mouth. Flesh and bone erupted out the back of the head.

The three kills had taken seconds.

Bolan waited until he was sure the guards' deaths had gone unnoticed. Then he moved out as silently as a flitting moth.

He slung the M-16 over his shoulder, stepped over the bodies and took a running leap at a low wall of the building.

He went up the wall easily, lithely.

When he reached the top, he lay flat.

No sounds came from the other side.

He had to chance it.

He swung himself down through the bomb-damaged roof into the building.

It was dark and still inside.

Nothing moved.

The fire outside cast a feeble glow down through the opening where the roof had once been.

As Bolan's eyes adjusted, he saw that the floor was littered with rubble from the collapsed roof. Moving carefully, he skirted the bigger chunks and made his way toward a heavy wooden door set in one wall.

The door was not fastened, just rested against the opening in the wall.

Bolan grabbed both edges of the door and shifted it sideways, creating a space just large enough to slip through.

Before him was a narrow corridor that was a little brighter than the room Bolan stepped from.

At the end of this hallway there was another door, which was ajar. The glow from a lantern filtered into the passageway. The floor of the hall was also covered with broken chunks of the roof.

Bolan padded along a pathway through the junk, taking great care not to set off a clatter, however slight.

As he had suspected, the hallway led to a main room at the front of the building. He stopped before he reached the door and flattened himself against the wall.

"You are a very stubborn woman," a man's heavily accented voice snarled.

"And you're a murderer of women and children."

Jill Desmond's voice was cold and flat and showed not a trace of the terror she must be feeling.

Bolan could not help but smile in the gloom.

Bullheaded she might be, but Jill Desmond, journalist, had guts.

"We can make things very unpleasant for you, Miss Desmond." The accented voice continued.

Has to be the VC leader, Bolan thought.

"If you will only cooperate with us, things will go much easier for you."

"Bullshit," live-wire Desmond shot back. "You'll do what you want anyway, no matter what I say. I won't give you the satisfaction of seeing me beg."

"That is regrettable." The VC sighed. "I must therefore summon assistance in this interrogation."

JILL WAS COLD.

Tropical country or not, she was cold. Fear made her that way.

She didn't have to be told what cooperate meant.

If she gave in, she would be smuggled north to Hanoi and made to parrot their line of garbage.

And garbage was what it was.

She knew that now.

They called themselves freedom fighters and patriots. No way. They were murderers, rapists, cold-blooded ravagers of the weak and defenseless.

Who was there to stop them?

The VC grunted his frustration. He grabbed Jill's hair, lacing his dirty fingers through her chestnut strands, and pulled cruelly, bringing a gasp of pain from her lips.

Then he gave her head a rough shove and stepped toward the door to call the torturers. The real interrogators.

Jill sensed movement behind her. She twisted her head to see what awful thing was going to happen next.

A tall young American soldier with chips-of-ice eyes stalked into the room.

Recognition flared in Jill's brain.

Sergeant Bolan!

The rifle in Bolan's hands spit death.

The round from the M-16 caught the VC leader in the throat. The man's neck disintegrated as blood splattered all over the room. The dead man tumbled and sprawled into a corner.

Jill Desmond, her fatigues torn but not indecently, sat tied in a crude wooden chair.

One quick step put Bolan beside the chair where Jill sat. Her eyes were wide, stunned, shocked by the violence she had seen and experienced tonight. But she was coherent. Bolan unsheathed his knife and cut the cord that bound her.

"You okay?" Bolan asked in an urgent whisper.

She took a deep ragged breath, then nodded.

"How did you find—"

Bolan interrupted the question with a gesture. "No time. Let's get out of here."

He walked to the dead officer and bent down. He rolled the corpse over and stripped the uniform jacket from it.

"Here," he snapped, and threw the garment to her.

Jill flinched from the jacket. It was specked with blood in places. But common sense and survival instinct prevailed over her revulsion.

She slipped into the jacket, knowing she would have to wear something over the torn fatigue tops or the jungle growth would flay her flesh to ribbons.

Bolan grasped the VC corpse and hauled it away from the door, shoving it against a wall where it would not be seen unless someone came all the way into the room. Then he extinguished the kerosene lantern that sat on a table.

In the last instant of light before the lantern went out, he saw Jill watching him. She was damned attractive, even after everything she had been through tonight.

He grasped her arm in the darkness.

"Come on."

He guided her into the narrow corridor that led to the back of the building.

She stumbled several times over the rubble, but Bolan's firm grip kept her from falling.

They had to hurry.

Much as he might have liked to take it easier for Jill's sake, they could not afford that luxury.

They had to get out of Xan Lung before the VC leader's body was discovered.

A startled shout echoed down the hallway, then harsh yells.

The body had been discovered.

Within seconds the chase would be on.

Bolan jerked Jill Desmond into the room at the end of the corridor of the damaged munitions dump. He pushed her toward the back wall.

"I'll give you a boost," he told her. "Once you're over, head for the tree line."

"What about you?" There was a genuine concern in her voice.

"I'll catch up to you," Bolan grunted.

He stooped and grasped her around the hips. He hoisted her into position so she would grab the top of the wall.

She started to pull herself up and over to the outside. Bolan placed one hand behind on a nicely shaped rump and gave a purely strategic push.

Jill hauled herself to the top. A second later she disappeared over the wall.

Bolan was right behind her.

He paused at the top of the wall.

There were several sections of the old munitions depot roof that were intact, though drooping, especially near the edge of the roof.

Bolan moved out onto one of those sections for a better look at the uproar gripping the Xan Lung camp.

The VC were disorganized. But only for the moment. Already someone had thrown more wood on the fire so that it blazed and shed stronger illumination across the jungle surrounding the clearing.

Time for the play, grandstand and all.

Last chance, in fact.

The blitz artist tugged grenades off his belt, moving smooth and efficiently, pulling out the pins one by one. He tossed the bundles of death and hellfire into the VC camp.

One Cong saw things dropping from the sky and let out a startled yell.

The first grenade blew and ripped him apart, leaving a shallow hole in the clay and a mangled splotch where a heartbeat before a man had stood.

One after another the grenades exploded.

Some of the VC dived for cover, but many of them never had a chance. Shrapnel tore into them, shredding lives and limbs in a fireworks display of airborne body parts. The air was filled with high-pitched screams as men died.

It took just seconds for Bolan's five grenades to unleash their hellfire. At least half a dozen VC died as the Executioner canceled their tabs.

That left quite a few of them alive. Some of them spotted Bolan.

Bolan flicked the M-16 to full-auto as the cooking muzzle tracked an arc of death. Bolan cut down three more of the enemy in a figure eight of blistering lead. They never knew what hit them. The 5.56mm slugs ripped through flesh, splattering brains, pulverizing hearts. Vietcong did weird death dances in the flickering firelight, before sprawling immobile into the dark shadows.

Bullets whizzed all around Bolan, singing angry songs near him.

From his position atop the wall he cast a glance toward the tree line where waist-high elephant grass bordered the jungle.

Jill had already vanished into the night.

Even if he never left this clearing, Jill would have a chance, he thought.

And that was all you could ask for in the jungle.

The M-16's muzzle spit its last round, planting a death kiss on the forehead of a Cong who had peeled off some rounds at Bolan from half-assed cover.

Bolan slung the rifle over his shoulder and grabbed for his holstered .45. But his weight suddenly became too much for the section of roof on which he perched.

With a rumble, it caved in.

Bolan fell with it.

As he dropped, he twisted his body in an instinctive reflex. His back scraped the top of the wall, but he fell outside the building.

He hit the ground, rolling, and came up ready to dive toward the back corner of the bombed-out arms depot.

Too far away.

His body would be butchered by VC slugs before he could cross the clearing.

"Hit the dirt!" a female voice yelled at him from somewhere beyond the flickering blaze.

Bolan hit the dirt, his .45 and eyes panning the night for targets.

He saw Jill come around the corner of the old munitions building with one of the fallen sentries' AK-47s. She held the rifle awkwardly, but there was nothing clumsy about the chattering stream of hot lead that erupted from its muzzle.

Bolan stayed prone under the line of fire and let the slugs chew up the careless enemy. Several went into stumbling death slides, blood spurting.

Bolan triggered his .45, adding to the carnage.

Jill reached his side and crouched there.

Their combined firepower, the lady journalist with her confiscated AK and marksman Bolan with the .45, was withering.

The smattering of answering fire from the darkness stuttered into nothing.

The jungle line was only a few meters away.

Bolan seized the lull, leathered his side arm and grabbed the lady's wrist, guiding her along with him as he withdrew for the tree line.

They plunged into the dark jungle undergrowth heedless of the branches and vines whipping at them like hungry things.

Jill let out a ragged breath from time to time, but Bolan urged her on. They could not afford to face more VC who might be in the vicinity.

Within moments, sounds of pursuit rustled in the distance behind them.

"Where did you learn to fire an assault rifle like that?" Bolan asked the woman.

"Back there," came the grim reply.

There was no trail through this part of the jungle, but they were heading in the general direction of the road from Three Click Fork.

Or so Bolan hoped.

His instincts proved right.

They stumbled out onto the rough surface of the road forty minutes later.

They would be better targets at the moment, if the VC managed to close in on them from behind, but they could move faster on the road.

The VC had not yet reached the road.

A shadow moved in front of them.

Bolan spun Jill away from him, splitting them up to make them harder targets. He brought up the reloaded M-16 and tracked the rifle on the moving spot.

His finger froze on the trigger a fraction of a second before sending a bullet into the night.

He heard the cry of a child.

A little boy, no more than four or five years old, stumbled into the road, tears running down his cheeks. His clothes were in tatters. There was blood on his face from a gash in his scalp.

He was alone.

Jill crouched on the other side of the road, her AK-47 up and ready. She saw the child, too, and moved back into the center of the road to join Bolan. He was already advancing toward the boy, more wary than ever of an enemy trap.

The child saw the two adults approaching and turned to run away.

Bolan caught the child's arm and stopped him.

Two still forms on the road nearby caught Bolan's attention. He took a closer look: the child's parents. Dead. Slaughtered.

"From that burned-out village, more than likely," Bolan grunted under his breath. "The

VC caught them on their way out. This is no place for the little guy. Not tonight.''

The soldier gathered the child up in his free arm and glanced at Jill.

She looked as if she needed to catch her breath, dangerous though the delay might be.

There was still no sign of Charlie.

Bolan let himself start to hope they might successfully escape.

"Take a minute," he told the woman. He looked at the boy and saw the terror on that young face. "It's okay, son. You'll be all right now." He patted the child.

The boy didn't understand the words, but Bolan's gestures reassured him. He stopped crying.

Jill watched the care and compassion with which Mack Bolan handled the Vietnamese youngster.

"Thank you," she said abruptly. "After everything I said to you earlier tonight, I don't know why you put your life on the line to save me."

"Orders," he said gruffly, grinning.

"I'm not so sure. I'm not sure about a lot of things I used to be very sure about."

"Like who the savages are?"

She grimaced.

"I think I was just introduced to them. What I saw...the atrocities they committed...that's what this war is all about, isn't it?''

"The families in that village were feeding us intel on VC movements," Bolan told her. "This war is about a lot of things, Jill. Some good, some bad, and all of it matters. I've learned a few things, too. I didn't figure anybody who felt like you do about this war could care enough to fight the way you just did. You are some lady, lady."

She met his eyes.

"I decided we were on the same side after all, soldier."

Bolan nodded.

Yeah, they were on the same side.

The side of humanity.

Bullets cracked past them.

The range was bad and so was the light, but the pursuing VC were peppering the night blindly from way back in the jungle as they closed in.

He and Jill jogged off beyond the tree line, away from approaching Vietcong.

At the sound of gunfire the child started squirming under Bolan's arm. He had seen home and family destroyed; innocent eyes witnessed what it was like when cannibals ran unchecked in the world.

A white-hot poker stabbed Bolan in the left leg.

He stumbled but did not go down. Not at first. Then the leg buckled, and he fell.

Bolan cradled the kid to prevent him from being hurt as he rolled over and got to one knee.

Jill stopped beside him, breathless from running.

He scanned the terrain behind them with combat-cold eyes, the M-16 ready. He handed the boy to Jill.

"Move!" he barked.

In the night their eyes met for a timeless moment. Then she ran off, clutching the little boy to her.

Bolan turned toward the direction of the pursuing VC.

Suddenly the jungle darkness blazed into brightness.

At first, Bolan did not see where it came from. There was no time to pinpoint the phosphorous flare that floated down from above.

He heard frantic scrambling noises close by. Squinting against the glare, he sent a long stream of hot lead into the wall of green made silver by the eerie glow of the flare.

Some of the scrambling and rustling sounds stopped. Some.

When the rifle's magazine ran dry, he barely paused in his firing to feed the M-16 a new clip so the mighty weapon could continue hammering, bucking in his steady grip.

It was then he realized the pounding wasn't in his veins but the rotor throb of an approaching chopper.

A big Huey gunship sailed into view overhead, its mounted machine guns raining death on the remaining VC.

Bolan got to his feet as the chopper settled down on the road. The heat of battle had made him forget the pain of his leg wound. Now it hurt like hell. His left leg was stiff from the gouge an enemy bullet had put there.

He looked around. Jill Desmond had stopped down the road a few hundred feet. He could make her out in the Huey's flight lights. She looked stunned.

Even the child was wide-eyed and quiet.

Blancanales called from the open door of the Huey.

"Move it, Sarge! We've got to get out of here before Charlie calls reinforcements."

The flare sputtered and died in the sky.

Jill Desmond ran over to Mack Bolan by the chopper.

Bolan took the kid from her and passed him up to Zitka's outstretched arms. He saw other members of Sniper Team Able inside the Huey.

"Must've read my mind," he said to them as he helped Jill into the gunship.

"You mean Colonel Crawford read your mind," Blancanales called above the rumble of the chopper's engine directly overhead. "The CO hit the ceiling when he found out you'd gone off on your own. Your butt is up for a chewing."

Bolan grinned as he climbed aboard.

"We'll see. Won't be the first time."

Gunsmoke was at the controls. "Still playing at Sergeant Mercy, huh, soldier?'' he called over in his Old West twang. ''God bless you, guy.''

Jill Desmond looked sharply at Bolan.

''Sergeant Mercy?''

''Sure,'' Blancanales said when Bolan made no reply. ''That's what all the Viet civilians call him. Didn't you know?''

''There's a lot of things I didn't know, soldier,'' the woman admitted, ''until tonight.''

The chopper's engine revved.

Bolan's hand found Jill's and squeezed. She returned the pressure. Feminine, yeah. Divinely so. But *hard*, too. The right stuff.

Bolan would be coming back.

Back to the job he did so well.

Back to the hellgrounds.

Sergeant Mercy.

The Executioner.

One man.

For now, though, that one man had earned a rest, however brief.

The chopper lifted off and banked up into the first light of a new day.

The future would take care of itself.

With a helping hand from Mack Bolan, as long as this soldier lived to fight the good fight.

Wherever it might take him.

ABLE TEAM

#11 Five Rings of Fire

MORE GREAT ACTION
COMING SOON

Able Team's creator, Mack "The Bastard" Bolan, is a fugitive once again, and Able Team's task becomes all the more thrilling as the Stony Man death squad battles to survive and to prevail against all subversion. The Los Angeles Olympic Games is the latest grim target of terror, and Able Team blazes into war to turn the traditional interlocked rings of sporting competition into flaming hoops of hellfire!

Watch for this major new novel in the continuing Able Team saga, and meet Mack Bolan, Leo Turrin, Carl Lyons and all the Stony Man people in future Gold Eagle adventures, presented by the very best writers in the business!

Available wherever paperbacks are sold.

Coming soon:

MACK BOLAN

Terminal Velocity

The new Super Bolan!
384 pages of electrifying adventure

Bolan, bereaved and all but beaten, stands in the shambles of Stony Man Farm.

The legendary warrior, whose sacred mission began in the jungles of Vietnam, and who came home to battle the savage mob in the urban jungle, now faces an even deadlier enemy.

A brilliantly conceived KGB trap lies in wait for him. The CIA has orders to kill him. And Mack the Blacksuit has no choice but to rise above all sanction. Betrayed and alone, he must strike at the very heart of the Hydra.

He must strike at Moscow.

This is Bolan's loneliest, deadliest war!

Now available:

SOBs

THE PLAINS OF FIRE
by Jack Hild

The Soldiers of Barrabas
bring justice to Iran!

Iran has the Bomb—and the zealots plan to use it for
international blackmail and for mass murder.

The United States government cannot intervene
without committing an act of war. But Nile Barrabas
and his SOBs are not the least bit shy when it comes to
acts of war. . . .

Their mission: to penetrate forbidden territory, search
out and destroy the heavily defended weapons
complex. And make it all look like an accident.

An atomic accident.

Mack Bolan's
PHOENIX FORCE
by Gar Wilson

Phoenix Force is The Executioner's five-man army that blazes through the dirtiest of encounters. Like commandos who fight for the love of battle and the righteous unfolding of the logic of war, Bolan's five hardasses make mincemeat out of their enemies. Catch up on the whole series now!

> "The hardest-hitting, highest-caliber he-man writing ever."
>
> —*Stag*

#1 **Argentine Deadline** #6 **White Hell**
#2 **Guerilla Games** #7 **Dragon's Kill**
#3 **Atlantic Scramble** #8 **Aswan Hellbox**
#4 **Tigers of Justice** #9 **Ultimate Terror**
#5 **The Fury Bombs**

Phoenix Force titles are available wherever paperbacks are sold.

What readers are saying about Able Team

"Action-packed! No other adventure series can hold a candle to Able Team. Keep up the good work!"
—*R.D.,*Caneyville, KY*

"Fast moving and full of action. If only they made movies like Stivers writes books!"
—*R.G., Newark, DE*

"The world needs men like Bolan and his hell-wringers, Able Team and Phoenix Force—men of justice and integrity! Your books are literary magic. I hope they stay around forever."
—*G.H., Smithers, BC*

"Your books are a reward at the end of a hard day. I love this kind of action!"
—*C.F., Gulfsport, FL*

"These gentlemen mean business. I'm with them all the way."
—*D.P., Weaverville, NC*

"Able Team brings power to ordinary people."
—*D.C., Plantersville, AL*

*Names available on request

GOLD EAGLE

HE'S EXPLOSIVE.
HE'S UNSTOPPABLE.
HE'S MACK BOLAN!

He learned his deadly skills in Vietnam...then put them to use by destroying the Mafia in a blazing one-man war. Now **Mack Bolan** is back to battle new threats to freedom, the enemies of justice and democracy—and he's recruited some high-powered combat teams to help. **Able Team**—Bolan's famous Death Squad, now reborn to tackle urban savagery too vicious for regular law enforcement. And **Phoenix Force**—five extraordinary warriors handpicked by Bolan to fight the dirtiest of anti-terrorist wars around the world.

Fight alongside these three courageous forces for freedom in all-new, pulse-pounding action-adventure novels! Travel to the jungles of South America, the scorching sands of the Sahara and the desolate mountains of Turkey. And feel the pressure and excitement building page after page, with nonstop action that keeps you enthralled until the explosive conclusion! Yes, Mack Bolan and his combat teams are living large...and they'll fight against all odds to protect our way of life!

Now you can have all the new Executioner novels delivered right to your home!

You won't want to miss a single one of these exciting new action-adventures. And you don't have to! Just fill out and mail the coupon following and we'll enter your name in the Executioner home subscription plan. You'll then receive four brand-new action-packed books in the Executioner series every other month, delivered right to your home! You'll get two **Mack Bolan** novels, one **Able Team** and one **Phoenix Force**. No need to worry about sellouts at the bookstore...you'll receive the latest books by mail as soon as they come off the presses. That's four enthralling action novels every other month, featuring all three of the exciting series included in The Executioner library. Mail the card today to start your adventure.

FREE! Mack Bolan bumper sticker.

When we receive your card we'll send your four explosive Executioner novels and, absolutely FREE, a Mack Bolan "Live Large" bumper sticker! This large, colorful bumper sticker will look great on your car, your bulletin board, or anywhere else you want people to know that you like to "Live Large." And you are under no obligation to buy anything—because your first four books come on a 10-day free trial! If you're not thrilled with these four exciting books, just return them to us and you'll owe nothing. The bumper sticker is yours to keep, FREE!

Don't miss a single one of these thrilling novels...mail the card now, while you're thinking about it. And get the Mack Bolan bumper sticker FREE!

BOLAN FIGHTS AGAINST ALL ODDS TO DEFEND FREEDOM!

Mail this coupon today!